Ryan White

B. Heather Mantler

This book is dedicated to those who will be and are frustrated by the ending.

CHAPTER ONE

Ryan slowly opened his eyes to see the sun peeking out from behind the clouds. After three weeks of rain, the sight of the sun made Ryan smile. That and the afterglow from last night. With that thought, Ryan rolled over. The other side of the bed was empty. Ryan sat up and looked around. Aside from signs that someone had slept on the other side of the bed, there was no Abigail.

"Abby?" Ryan called. There was no answer. Ryan climbed out of bed and grabbed a pair of jeans off the floor. He pulled them on before going into the hallway. The bathroom door was open and there was no sign of Abigail, so Ryan moved to the kitchen. She wasn't there either. He checked the living room just to be sure, but as he figured she wasn't there. Everything was the same mess as it was the night before, except that her clothing and belongings were gone.

Ryan went back to the bedroom and looked around.

Abigail's clothes were gone. Ryan opened the drawers in the dresser and found each one was empty. Ryan ended up sitting down against the bed. He put his hands through his hair as he rested his forehead on his knee.

Just when he thought he had found happiness, it disappears. But this time, there were no hints Abigail would leave him. Abigail had seemed just as happy as he was. She didn't even leave a note explaining why she left. And he had no idea how to get a hold of her to ask why.

The phone rang. Ryan scrambled to grab it off the dresser. He knocked the phone to the floor, but managed to grab the receiver.

"Hello?" Ryan tried to keep the hope out of his voice.

"Dude, are you okay?" Tony asked with concern in his voice.

"No," Ryan answered, "What do you want?"

"Audrey kicked me out again," Tony said, "Got a couch I can stay on, or are you busy using it with Abby? Everything is still okay with Abby, right?"

"I wouldn't know," Ryan said, "She seems to have disappeared."

"Maybe she went out to the corner store for provisions," Tony said, "Audrey does that sometimes without telling me."

"Does she take all her stuff with her?" Ryan asked.

"Since she owns all the furniture," Tony said, "No."

"Abby doesn't take her stuff with when she goes to the store, either," Ryan said.

"What did the note say?" Tony asked, "It has to be better than the one Kayla left."

"I haven't found a note," Ryan answered.

"That really sucks," Tony said, "To leave and not even tell you why. But at least you have a free couch to let a friend stay on."

"I'm not sure I'm up to having anyone over," Ryan said.

"Come on," Tony said, "I'll meet you at the Tavern and we can drink away any thoughts of all women."

"What did you do to get Audrey angry at you?" Ryan asked.

"I've got the tab," Tony said, "Don't worry about it."

"I'll see you at the Tavern," Ryan said before putting the receiver back and putting the phone back on the dresser. He grabbed the shirt off the floor and was just about to put it on when he smelled Abigail on it. Ryan tossed it in the direction of the laundry basket. He went to the other side of the bed and opened the top drawer. He grabbed the top shirt and pulled it on.

The thought that the shirt was Abigail's favourite hit him as he searched for his keys. He pushed it to one side and kept searching for his keys. He found them on the kitchen floor below the picture of an ocean scene that needed to be straightened. Ryan pushed that thought away as well.

Ryan left the apartment and locked the door behind him. He headed down the street to the Tavern. The door was locked, so Ryan knocked on the glass. A moment passed before Lucas opened the door and looked at Ryan.

"Tony said he would pay for it," Ryan said.

"Okay," Lucas said, "But if either of you pukes in here, I'm charging extra."

"I fine with that," Ryan said. Lucas opened the door

enough for Ryan to enter before locking it again.

"I thought you had a good relationship happening," Lucas said as he led the way to the bar.

"She disappeared last night without so much as a note explaining why," Ryan sat down on the stool.

"Ouch," Lucas said as he poured Ryan a beer.

"Yeah," Ryan said, "Just when I thought I had found my perfect ten."

"I didn't think you were much into rating girls," Lucas said.

"I have a ten-point system to help me find the right girl," Ryan said, "The perfect girl for me has to have a good sense of humour, be friendly with my friends, kind to strangers, not a doormat, not a mother figure, good looking, looking for a partnership, fun to be with, good in bed, and doesn't take life too seriously. Abby was all that and so much more. Happiest six months of my life and the flames never diminished."

Lucas refilled the empty glass with beer.

"I can't remember any hints that she was unhappy or wanted out. She could tell me about anything and I would do my best to accept it. I almost think that she would be there still sleeping if I went back to my apartment, but she took all her stuff with her. There is nothing left, except for her scent. And that is going to drive me nuts if I don't get around to cleaning soon."

Lucas nodded as he refilled the beer. Ryan kept drinking as he talked about his problem to Lucas. He was into his fifth beer before Tony knocked on the glass. Lucas let him in and poured them both a beer. Ryan started all over again for Tony's benefit and Lucas got on with what he needed to do to open for the evening. He occasionally stopped on his way passed and refill their drinks.

By the time the staff arrived for the night, Ryan and Tony had packed away a lot of beer. They were having problems staying on their stools when Lucas opened the Tavern. At nine, Lucas kicked them out as too drunk to serve. Ryan and Tony leaned on each other as they staggered back to Ryan's apartment.

Ryan managed to get the key in the lock on the second try. They went inside giggling over themselves. Tony closed the door. Ryan made his way to the bedroom, tripping over things left on the floor from the night before. The last thing he tripped over was a coat. He found he couldn't get up and instead crawled the rest of the way into the bedroom. He got an arm's length from the bed and stopped to pass out.

There was throbbing behind his eyes, as Ryan became conscious of the carpet beneath him. His tongue felt fuzzy and he wasn't sure if he had woken up in the right body. He wanted to curl into a fetal position and have the pain go away, but there was light poking at his eyes as if to try and wake him up.

Ryan let his eyes open, but everything looked blurry, so he closed them again. There was a noise from somewhere else in the apartment of a person cussing. It vibrated in Ryan's head and if he could move, he might have put his hands over his ears. Ryan opened his eyes again. The carpet fibres were much more in focus now, but everything else was still blurry. Ryan closed his eyes again. The cussing person was moving toward the hallway. They kicked the coat out of the way and cursed it. They staggered into the bathroom and the door slammed. Ryan groaned as he winced. If he lived through this, he was going to kill the person making all that noise.

Ryan opened his eyes again. He could now see the corner of the quilt that hung off the bed and a blue piece of cloth under the bed. Ryan reached out, picked up the blue fabric, and pulled it out to better look at it. It was Abby's underwear. The only pair she owned. The pair she washed out in the sink and hung to dry on the towel rod every night. Something was wrong and when Ryan's brain was cleared of all the cobwebs, he was sure he would figure it out.

The sound of running water came from the bathroom, causing Ryan to scrunch the underwear up in his hand and rolled over. He wasn't sure that there was anything in his stomach to throw up, but he had to stifle the reflex. He looked around. There was light coming from the window, but it was impossible to tell what time of day it was. The room was how he remembered leaving it yesterday to go meet Tony at the Tavern.

Tony was the person in the bathroom making so much noise. Ryan was going to kill him if he could ever move without aching. Ryan closed his eyes again to see if that would stop the headache a little. It didn't, but it felt slightly better. Maybe he could lie like this for a couple more hours everything would be okay. Ryan became aware of his bladder demanding to release all the beer he had drunk last night. And it would prefer to do so now, rather than later.

Tony opened the bathroom door with more noise than necessary before stumbling down the hallway toward the living room with the noise of an elephant stampede. Ryan opened his eyes and slowly sat up. He stopped briefly to stifle the urge to puke before moving on to the next step. He used the bed and the dresser drawers to get to his feet. He swayed like a palm tree before a storm but made it to the doorway without falling. Ryan reached across the hallway for the bathroom doorway before letting go of the bedroom doorway. In the bathroom, he used the counter and the shower bar. When he reached the toilet, Ryan sighed with relief as he let his bladder go.

When he was finished, Ryan kept himself upright to flush the toilet, wash his hands, and stumble back to the bedroom. He could hear Tony in the living room but didn't care as long as nothing was destroyed. Ryan found the bed and collapsed into it. He barely closed his eyes before he was snoring again.

"Dude," Tony's voice came from the doorway. Ryan moved his head that direction and then opened his eyes. The fogginess of his brain lifted enough to remind him of the massive headache that was there.

"Dude, it is like supper time," Tony said, "You slept all day."

"And if felt so much better to be asleep," Ryan replied.

"I had to take your phone messages," Tony said.

"Any from Abby?" Ryan asked.

"No," Tony said, "But your mother called."

"If it wasn't Abby, I don't care," Ryan said. Tony entered the bedroom.

"Come on, Dude," Tony said, "You have to rejoin the land of the living."

"Why?" Ryan asked.

"Dude, what's in your hand?" Tony said looking at Ryan's left hand. Ryan looked over at it. There was blue fabric in it. He brought it closer to his face. It was a pair of underwear. The memory of it being under the bed was quickly overrun by his memory taking them off Abigail.

"Whose underwear did you find?" Tony was now close enough to see what it was.

"Abby's," Ryan answered.

"She left a pair of underwear behind?" Tony asked, "What is it? Some sort of joke?"

"She didn't see them because they were under the bed," Ryan said as he blocked out the memories to focus on the problem nagging at him, "I'm not sure why she wouldn't have searched harder for them."

"She didn't want to wake you," Tony suggested.

"She didn't own any other pairs," Ryan said.

"Maybe it is like when a girl leaves her favourite thing behind so that she can come back and get it," Tony said, "Maybe she'll call looking for it soon."

"She has been a day without underwear," Ryan said, "At what point do you just buy another pair and move on, because I doubt she would come back when she couldn't be bothered to leave a note the first time she left."

"I don't know," Tony said, "But I wouldn't suggest you take it to bed with you every night."

"Out of my room," Ryan said, "I can be dead to the world for a few hours more."

"But what about supper?" Tony asked.

"I said out and I meant out," Ryan said. Tony made a puppy face before backing up in the direction of the door. Ryan just pointed to the hallway. Tony closed the door on his way out.

Ryan let go of the underwear before slowly sitting

up. His head still hurt, but there was no urge to puke this time. He glanced out the window. The sun was hidden by clouds making it look later than Tony had said. Ryan glanced at the clock. It said five pm.

Ryan put his head in his hands to try a keep it from falling apart. As he did so, the rain started to hit the window. At least now, the weather matched his mood. Ryan got to his feet and went to lean against the window frame. Outside everything that had dried out was drenched again. Not that long ago, Ryan wouldn't have minded the rain because he and Abigail would spend the day in bed. Without Abigail, Ryan didn't know what to do with the day. He could leave the room and spend the day with Tony, which didn't appeal to Ryan.

For the last year, Tony hadn't been all that fun to be around and Ryan didn't want to know the problem. The night Ryan met Abigail, Tony had been too busy drinking away his problems with his girlfriend and left Ryan to find his own amusement. Ryan took Jey's invitation to join his band, Smash, backstage after their show. Jey and his girlfriend, Savanna, were sitting on the couch with Abigail. Savanna and Abigail were laughing and trading advice on wearing a short skirt, of which both had on. Abigail was also wearing a top that showed her lack of bra while still leaving enough to the imagination. Her brown hair had been pulled back in a classy bun, which showed off her silver, dangling earrings.

Ryan had practically fallen for her at first sight, only experience of what usually happened when he fell had kept his feet in reality. Jey had introduced them before inviting Ryan to join them on the couch. Ryan had hesitated at first because there hadn't been much room, but Savanna had moved to Jey's lap to give him space. Apparently, Abigail had liked him as well because she took up residence in his bed for the next three days and he happily stayed beside her. She explained that she was between jobs and apartments at the moment and needed someplace to stay until she could get enough money together to move along. Except she had never found a job and she was more than happy to stay with him.

Ryan looked over at the phone. Jey may have heard from Abigail, after all, he had introduced them. Ryan went over to the phone and picked up the receiver. He dialled Jey's number and waited as it rang.

"Hello?" Savanna's voice came over the phone.

"It's Ryan," Ryan said, "Is Jey there?"

"He's got a show tonight," Savanna answered, "I can take a message, or you can meet with him after the show."

"Where is the show tonight?" Ryan asked.

"The Ballroom," Savanna answered.

"Sounds high class," Ryan said, "How high is the cover charge?"

"Go in by the back door and Oscar will let you in," Savanna said, "I'll call and let him know you are coming."

"Thanks," Ryan said.

"See you there," Savanna said. She put the phone down. Ryan hung up the receiver. He went across the hallway to the bathroom. When he was finished, he changed into clothing more suited for a Smash show. When he came out to the kitchen for some water and painkillers, Ryan found Tony sitting in the living room eating one of the pizzas out of the freezer.

"Where are you going?" Tony glanced up from his show to look at Ryan.

"The Ballroom to talk to Jey," Ryan answered.

"Glad you are going to join the living," Tony said as he turned back to his show.

"And when are you going to go back to living?" Ryan asked.

"I'm living," Tony said.

"You are sitting on my couch, eating pizza, and watching reality TV shows," Ryan said, "You're in denial and it isn't going to help you any."

Ryan made sure he had his keys and wallet before leaving the apartment. He caught a cab a few streets over and was on his way.

The cab dropped him off at the stage door. Ryan got out, went to the door, and knocked. A moment passed before the door was opened by a brick wall of a man. The man looked Ryan over.

"Hello, Oscar," Ryan said.

"Savanna said you were coming," Oscar moved so that could Ryan enter.

"How's the show going?" Ryan asked.

"Quite well," Oscar answered, "There is even the possibility that they will get a contract for an album if they are good enough tonight."

"They must have started pretty early," Ryan followed Oscar through the backstage area.

"Show started at four and goes until nine with a half an hour break at seven," Oscar said, "They weren't sure about the length, but they agreed to it. I think the guy just wants to know that they have enough songs for an album without resorting to covers. He'll learn that they will run out of night before they run out of songs."

"They should do fine," Ryan said.

"You wanna wait back here," Oscar asked, "Or you want to sit in the booth and hear them play."

"Might as well hear them play," Ryan said.

"This way," Oscar led the way around to a private booth and they both sat down. Oscar already had a drink on the table. He pointed to it and raised an eyebrow. Ryan shook his head and concentrated on the band. They were fully involved in giving the best show they could. Ryan relaxed and let the music be his focus.

At seven, the band took a break and the room lights were turned on to let people get up. The bathroom would be a popular place for the next half an hour. Oscar went backstage and left Ryan in the booth. Five minutes later, Jey slid into the booth.

"First time I have seen you alone in six months," Jey commented.

"That is why I'm here," Ryan said, "Abby disappeared with all her belongings before I woke up yesterday morning. I was wondering if you knew where she might go."

"She upset with you?" Jey asked.

"Not that I know of," Ryan answered.

"She upset with something else?" Jey asked.

"Not that I know of," Ryan answered, "She seemed happy the night before she disappeared."

"Gonna try to talk her into coming back?" Jey asked.

"Or at least give her back the underwear she left behind," Ryan answered.

"She left her only pair of underwear at your place?"

Jey asked, "That's bizarre. Savanna told me about her only having one pair. I asked why she didn't buy another and Savanna said something about it being hard to find a pair she likes. Abby and Savanna were supposed to go shopping tomorrow for clothing."

"Did Abby cancel?" Ryan asked.

"Not that I know of," Jey answered, "But I don't know where she would go if she isn't with you. Savanna brought her to the show where you met her. I didn't know her before that. Savanna hasn't said anything about where she met Abby. Savanna doesn't talk much about before we met and she tells me that it is better that I don't know. I've learned that happiness is listening over knowledge."

"Savanna was coming later?" Ryan asked.

"Any time now," Jey answered, "What took you so long to come talk to me?"

"Tony dragged me out for a drink yesterday," Ryan said, "Slept through most of the hangover."

"Tony has a problem," Jey said.

"Apparently," Ryan said.

"I'll see if Savanna is here," Jey said before sliding out of the booth. He went backstage and Ryan was left alone again.

It was ten minutes later that Oscar and Savanna slid into the booth.

"Jey said you wanted to ask about Abby," Savanna said.

"She disappeared yesterday morning," Ryan said, "And I was hoping you knew where I could find her."

"She hasn't called me," Savanna said, "So, I don't know where she is. We are supposed to go shopping tomorrow. I can ask her what happened then."

"And ask her if she wants her underwear back," Ryan said.

"She forgot her underwear?" Savanna asked.

"I found it under the bed," Ryan replied.

"That's weird, but I'll ask about it," Savanna said, "She usually doesn't leave like that."

"How long have you known her?" Ryan asked.

"Three years," Savanna answered, "We met at a concert when we were both between boyfriends. We rented an apartment together for three months. After that, I moved in with a guy and I lost track of Abby for a while before we met up again a year and a half later. She was between jobs again and needed someplace to stay. I had an apartment with a group of other girls. She stayed there for about three weeks and then there was a strange phone call. Someone else picked it up, but the person was asking for her. She packed up and left immediately after. I didn't see her again until six months ago when she walked into the bar where the show was. She was happy with you, so there must be some other reason why she left."

"If there is a reason, I would like to know," Ryan said, "She didn't leave a note or anything."

"I'll get her to phone you if possible," Savanna said.

"Okay," Ryan said.

"The show is starting," Oscar said. They were quiet as the band came back on and just sat listening to the music.

Ryan woke to the sound of a daytime talk show. He looked over at Abigail's side of the bed as if expecting her to have shown up just like she disappeared. It was still empty and the talk show host was talking to a kidnapping victim. The victim had been eight years old when she was kidnapped by her father's former mistress. It took ten years before the police tracked the woman down and rescued the girl. By then, the girl had given up the thought of rescue and now had to go through therapy to adapt back into her life. A therapist took over in talking about all the hurdles there were in getting back to normal.

Ryan climbed out of bed and pulled on clothes before going out to the living room. Tony was sitting there eating a bowl of cereal and watching the show.

"You'll go deaf if you have the volume up that loud," Ryan said.

"Why would I go deaf?" Tony asked, "It isn't like I'm listening with headphones."

"Because I'm going to scream in your ear in the middle of the night until you are," Ryan said, "After all, if you can't keep the volume down when I'm trying to sleep, why should I let you sleep."

"All you had to do was ask," Tony grumbled as he turned the volume down.

"It is already too late today," Ryan said before going into the kitchen to make himself breakfast.

"You weren't exactly quiet when you were dropped off last night," Tony said as he followed Ryan, "You were drunk again."

"I enjoyed the show," Ryan said, "and you were busy draining your brain cells with TV. I think you need to buy a gift for Audrey and apologize for whatever you did that caused her to kick you out. Either that or you need to find your own apartment."

"You're kicking me out too?" Tony asked, "Some friend you are."

"You have been a downer for a year now," Ryan said, "When I'm already feeling bad about Abby leaving me, I don't need your pity party on my couch. So, you can stay if you cheer up and turn off the TV, or you can find another friend to bother."

Tony stared at Ryan in surprise, but didn't say anything. Ryan made himself breakfast as he waited for a response.

By the time Ryan was sitting down to eat, Tony finally came out of shock. Tony emptied his bowl, stuck it in the dishwasher, and then went into the living room. The TV shut off, there was some rustling, and then the door was slammed behind him. Ryan continued to eat.

After he cleaned up from breakfast, Ryan sat down in the chair beside the window. He watched the world go by as he waited for the phone to ring. Ryan knew that Savanna wouldn't be up before noon, so shopping wouldn't start until one at least. He just wasn't sure what to do with himself until then. He had no interest in daytime TV. He also didn't have any work that he had to get done. Going out meant that he could miss the phone call. Ryan felt like his whole life was hanging on that phone call.

Noon arrived and Ryan got up. He went into the kitchen and made himself lunch. He had just finished cleaning up when there was a knock on his door. Ryan went and looked through the eyehole. He was expecting it to be Tony back to beg to stay, but instead, it was Savanna. She looked agitated. Ryan opened the door and held it for Savanna to enter. She was clasping her hands and chewing on her lip as she stepped inside. Ryan closed the door and motioned for her to come into the kitchen. She went and sat down on one of the stood beside the island.

"Can I get you anything?" Ryan asked.

"Got anything hard to drink?" Savanna asked.

"Rum," Ryan answered.

"Straight, please," Savanna said. Ryan poured a glass of rum and set it in front of Savanna. Savanna took a long gulp before setting the glass down. She didn't finish it, so Ryan didn't offer to refill it.

"I showed up where we were supposed to meet," Savanna said, "Abby wasn't there. I texted her to ask if she was running late. The text came back as undeliverable, so I called her cell. The message said that the number was no longer in service. Which is completely weird for Abby. No matter where she moves, she keeps her cell. So that kinda freaked me out, but I still wanted to get to the sale at Marty's. I was gonna come back and see if she showed up late. Marty's sale was fine, but I couldn't find anything like what I was looking for. But when I came out of Marty's, I noticed these two guys in suits standing near the plant pots looking around as if searching for someone specific. I headed back to the food court. As I went, I noticed that the men in suits were following me. I tried to lose them, but they always seemed to know where I was. I had to shut off my cell before they quit showing up whenever I turned around.

"They didn't follow me here, or at least I never saw them. But seeing them and everything makes me think that Abby is in trouble. Her leaving without a word in the middle of the night when she was happy, disconnecting her cell, and then the guys in suits. There is something wrong. We need to find her."

"So, where do we start looking?" Ryan asked, "She told me very little about her history. And is there a possibility that she is just in hiding from the men in the suits? After all, they could have been following you thinking you could lead them to Abby. Last night you said that she ran when someone called looking for her."

"She would have woken you up and told you she couldn't stay," Savanna said, "She told us that she had to leave and she wouldn't be back. She cared about you, so she wouldn't have left without a word, even if she was worried about someone after her. She was kidnaped."

"But it wasn't the men in suits?" Ryan asked.

"I don't know," Savanna answered, "They could just be around to make sure they didn't miss anything."

"How do we find her if she was taken by men in suits?" Ryan asked.

"Follow her cell," Savanna answered.

"I don't have the resources to get information on her cell," Ryan said, "Unless you do."

"Jey once hired this great PI to help him out with finding someone," Savanna said, "I don't have the money without borrowing it from Jey, but you have money for it."

"I have a little bit of money I can use," Ryan said, "But I would have to take a couple of jobs to keep my current level of living."

"Is that a problem?" Savanna asked, "I don't know that much about what you do."

"I have several jobs that have been sitting there waiting for me, but I really haven't wanted to touch them," Ryan said, "I do those and any other urgent jobs to have more than enough for the PI. Do you have the number for the PI?"

"I don't know," Savanna said as she put her purse on the counter. She opened it and started pawing through it. Ryan didn't think that much stuff could fit in that small a purse and still close. She went back through the stuff.

"Not in there?" Ryan asked.

"I need to get the business card from Jey," Savanna said, "Or at least the phone number. Can I use your phone?"

"Sure," Ryan picked up the cordless and handed it to Savanna. Savanna started to dial the number.

"If the men in suits are following me through my cell," Savanna said as she waited for Jey to pick up, "Do you think they might have your phone tapped?"

"If they managed to kidnapped Abby in the middle of the night, the whole place could be bugged," Ryan said, "We'll have to ask the PI about checking for them."

"Yeah," Savanna said, "Now that we have discussed the whole situation here."

"That just means they'll be a couple steps ahead of us," Ryan said. Savanna nodded.

"Jey," Savanna said into the phone, "Can I get the number of the PI you used? I'm hoping that the PI can help find Abby." Savanna pulled a pen and piece of paper out of her purse and started writing down a phone number. "His name is Hagan, okay. Yeah, I know. Also, can you get someone to come and pick me up? I'm at Ryan's place. Thanks." Savanna hit the button to hang up the phone before handing it back to Ryan.

"Here's the number for Hagan the PI," Savanna said turning the paper toward Ryan.

"Thanks," Ryan said before dialling the number on the paper. It rang a dozen times before the answering machine asked for Ryan's name and reason for calling. "This is Ryan White. I'm looking to hire you to find someone. Call me back at 555-6789 if you have time." The beep ended the message and Ryan pressed the button to hang up the phone.

"How long do you think it'll take for him to get back to me?" Ryan asked Savanna.

"I guess it has to do with how busy he is," Savanna answered, "Jey dealt with him, not me, so I don't really know."

"He'll want to talk to you about where Abby has been at some point," Ryan said.

"Get him to call and set up a time," Savanna said, "I will help as much as I can."

"Get your cell checked over," Ryan said, "You might even have to replace it."

"Jey knows a guy who can help with that," Savanna said.

"Jey knows plenty of people who can help with that sort of thing," Ryan said, "And they are all old friends willing to do favours for him. I found that out a long time ago."

"We don't discuss history," Savanna said, "It only comes up if the need does." Savanna threw back the rest of the rum and put the glass back on the counter. Ryan picked up the bottle to offer her some more, but Savanna shook her head.

"Thanks for the drink," Savanna said, "It helped after havin' those men in suits chasing me around the mall. That was freaky and now I'm scared for Abby. I can't imagine how she got herself involved with such people, but it can't end well for her. We need to find her before anything further happens to her. She needs us." Savanna stuffed everything back into her purse and closed it. Her hands had started shaking again. Ryan poured a mouthful of rum into the glass. Savanna gave him half a smile before downing the drink. It calmed her down a bit.

"I should check to see if my ride is here yet," Savanna said.

"The living room window shows the road out front," Ryan said, "You can look out there."

"Thanks," Savanna said as she got off the stool. She went out to the living room. Ryan looked down at the phone on the counter. He willed it to ring, but it remained silent. He placed back in its base and put the rum back in the cupboard before setting the glass in the dishwasher.

"There's my ride," Savanna called from the living room. She came back into the kitchen. "Let me know how things go."

"I will," Ryan said as he saw her to the door. Once she was outside, Ryan went to the living room window. The car sitting at the curb was the keyboard player's car and Jey was standing outside. He waved to Ryan and Ryan waved back. Savanna came into sight. She and Jey got into the back seat and the door closed. Savanna stuck her arm out the window and waved to Ryan before the car drove away.

Ryan watched it until it was out of sight before turning back towards the kitchen. At that moment, the phone rang. Ryan dashed to the kitchen and grabbed the cordless. He just about forgot to push the button.

"Hello?" it was a little breathless.

"This is Hagan, the PI," the male voice said, "A Ryan White from this number left a message."

"I'm Ryan and I want to hire you," Ryan said.

"What's the case?" Hagan asked.

"I need you to find my missing girlfriend," Ryan answered.

"Have you tried the police?" Hagan asked.

"No," Ryan answered, "Because they wouldn't believe me, or they would ignore it."

"I charge a hundred dollars cash to listen to the case," Hagan said, "A two hundred retainer if I think I can help you."

"Where would you like to meet and discuss the case?" Ryan asked.

"There is a coffee shop at the corner of 7th Avenue and Willow Street," Hagan said, "Half an hour."

"I'll have to stop at the bank first," Ryan said, "How about forty-five minutes?"

"Fine," Hagan said, "I'll be seated in the back with a black fedora."

"I'll see you there," Ryan said. Hagan hung up the phone. Ryan put the phone back on its base.

Ryan hurried through the apartment making sure that he had his wallet, keys, and jacket. It hadn't rained yet today, but the clouds threatened. Ryan locked the door of his apartment before heading down the street to the bank machine.

Once he had the cash, Ryan called a cab to take him to the coffee shop.

The cab dropped him out front before going off to find another customer. Ryan watched it go before looking at the coffee shop. It was one of those places that advertised a dozen organic roasts and half the people passing through looked homeless. There were enough business people that Ryan wouldn't look out of place. The place was also fairly busy, but most people didn't stop to enjoy the coffee so there were plenty of free tables.

Ryan checked his watch. He was on time. He went inside and looked around. There was a man at a table in the back wearing a black fedora. He also had a mustache that looked like it had to be fake because it didn't match his hair. His coat matched the hat, but the jeans looked grubby. The man's grey eyes watched as Ryan walked across the coffee shop and sat down in the chair across from him.

Ryan placed the envelope with the hundred dollars on the table. Hagan didn't even check the contents before slipping it into his jacket.

"Jey's girlfriend said you found someone that Jey was looking for," Ryan said, "I'm hoping you can do that same for me."

"And yet, the police wouldn't be able to help you?" Hagan asked.

"I woke up two days ago and found my girlfriend, Abigail Ward, gone," Ryan said, "All of her belongings were gone as well, except her only pair of underwear which was out of sight under the bed. There was no note or any explanation. She was happy before that and gave no indication that she would leave. Today she was supposed to go shopping with Jey's girlfriend, who is her friend, but she didn't show up. Savanna called her cell and found that it was no longer connected."

"None of this seems worth looking in to," Hagan said, "But I can understand why you can't call the police. They wouldn't look into either."

"And I might pass it off as she left of her own will," Ryan said, "But two men in suits showed up and followed Savanna around the mall after she had tried to contact Abby. I've known Abby for six months and she never quite seemed like the type to just take off without telling at least Savanna."

"She could have been found by a bad element from her past and needed to get out in a hurry," Hagan said, "Wouldn't be the first time."

"She would tell Savanna," Ryan said, "Abby would find a payphone on the way out of town, or at the first place she stopped. If she didn't go to Savanna for help to start with. It is the men in the suits that suggest there is more going on."

"That is a little strange," Hagan said, "You sure they weren't after Savanna? Savanna does have her own history."

"Anything that would merit men in suits?" Ryan asked.

"Not that I have found," Hagan answered, "I'll look into your girlfriend's history, but if I find that it is most likely that she just ran off, I'll cut off the investigation."

"But if there is anything strange, you will continue to investigate?" Ryan asked.

"I will," Hagan said.

"Then you can have you two hundred dollars when you bring the contract around," Ryan said.

"I accept those terms," Hagan said.

"Good," Ryan stood up.

"Not going to give me an address to bring the contract?" Hagan asked.

"You're the investigator," Ryan said, "If you can't find me then you're not worth the money." Ryan walked away from Hagan and left the coffee shop. He thought about getting another cab, but decided to walk instead. It might rain on him, but he would spend less time sitting around his apartment missing Abby.

CHAPTER TWO

The next day Ryan had gotten up and looked over the job offers in his inbox. There were a couple good ones, but a few not so good ones that he would have to do to keep the money coming in while he went off on this search. He responded to all of them to say that he would take the job and needed all the information about the situation before he could help them.

Ryan had just finished all that when there was a knock at the door to the apartment. He went and looked through the eyehole. Hagan was standing there in the same hat and coat as the day before, but the fake mustache was gone. He had a backpack with him. Ryan unlocked the door and opened it.

"It wasn't difficult to find you," Hagan said.

"Come in," Ryan said. Hagan stepped inside and Ryan closed the door. Ryan waved Hagan toward the kitchen. Hagan took the room in as he entered it and then sat down on the stool Savanna had occupied the day before. He took out a piece of paper and set it on the counter.

"Savanna suggested yesterday that they bugged the place when they took Abby," Ryan said, "And I have no way of telling."

"She could be paranoid," Hagan said.

"I accept that explanation, too," Ryan said.

"Sign here," Hagan took out a pen and pointed to the line at the bottom. Ryan took the pen, but skimmed the contract before signing his name. Hagan separated the carbon paper copy and gave it to Ryan. Ryan folded it up and put it in his pocket.

"I have the equipment to check for bugs," Hagan said, "I'll do that before we go any further."

"Go ahead," Ryan said.

Hagan nodded and took out a handheld machine. He turned it on and started wandering around the apartment with it. Ryan wandered from room to room as Hagan did.

It took about half an hour for Hagan to finish with the handheld machine and sit back down on the stool.

"There are no bugs in the apartment," Hagan said, "I'll test your phone line before I leave, but be careful what you say over the phone anyways. If I start digging, they may put the tap on later."

"So, you believe that there is someone out there," Ryan said.

"I did some digging last night," Hagan said, "I didn't think it would hurt and it would tell me whether this would be an interesting case. Abigail Ward has been travelling around for about seven years, barely staying anywhere for more than ten months. She has kept the same name, but it pops up like she crosses the country each time she moves on. Most of the time there isn't much for official records of her, just people she was friends with who she keeps in touch with or leaves behind as things work out. Savanna is a good example of that.

"However, official records of Abigail Ward report her as dying less than six months after she was born. She was born premature and the clinic near where her mother lived didn't have the necessary equipment to help her. Her fifteen-year-old mother had no money to go to a hospital and get the proper care. Abigail Ward is buried on community funds with a simple marker. Her mother, Natalie Ward, committed suicide a year later and I haven't found any living relatives.

"The ID for Abigail Ward was created seven years ago by a man called Flint. He is an expert in making realistic IDs and giving people new identities. I spoke with him and asked about Abigail. She was introduced to him by a bartender who he used many times to get clients. Abigail refused to give him any name before he handed her the new identity. The bartender disappeared two years after the introduction. He was abducted and tortured. His body washed up on the edge of a river near the city where he had lived. The police never solved the case and haven't had one like it since. Though the police theorized that his death was an accident and the abductors didn't get the information they wanted. After seeing the autopsy report, I would agree with them.

"Abigail Ward then showed up at a retail store across the country. She never had a boyfriend there, but she did share the apartment with three other girls. She stayed there for four months. She left because she was fired from her job and was having trouble finding another one. For most of those seven years, it was that kind of thing that caused her to move on. Until a year and a half ago when she received a phone call while staying with friends when she packed up and left without any other reason.

"I'm still waiting to get a hold of the telephone records from that phone call, as well as the records for her cell and your phone records. When I call Savanna, I will ask for her cell and records."

"Can you figure out who she was before she became Abigail Ward?" Ryan asked.

"Can I get fingerprints and DNA for her?" Hagan asked.

"If you can find them," Ryan answered.

"How often do you clean in here?" Hagan asked as he pulled a kit out of his backpack.

"Last time was three or four weeks ago," Ryan answered, "And that was only because the dust was getting to me."

"When I'm finished, I'm going to need a copy of your prints for elimination purposes," Hagan said.

"That's fine," Ryan said.

"Now, let's see what can be found," Hagan said as he took powder and a brush out of the kit. He started scrutinizing the surfaces in the kitchen.

Ryan followed him through the apartment as Hagan searched for siutable surfaces to get prints. When Hagan found one he would dust it, but aside from a few places that Ryan remembered touching recently, or seeing Tony touch, there were no prints. They went through the whole apartment and Hagan got annoyed at the lack of prints.

"Whoever took Abigail wiped everything down," Hagan said when they arrived back in the kitchen, "It doesn't look like I'm going to get any prints. Next to see if they did the same with DNA."

Ryan again followed Hagan as he went around looking for traces of Abby. He didn't find much for useful hairs, so he pulled apart the pipes under the bathroom sink in the bathroom to see if he could get hair from in there. He had it apart and brought it close to his nose before shaking his head.

"Bleach," Hagan said as he put the pipe back together, "They poured bleach down the drain and that means any hair is useless. Whoever these people are, they were thorough about getting rid of her from your apartment and quiet about. I don't think I'm going to get anything that will help me identify her here."

"There may be one place that they didn't get," Ryan said suddenly remembering something.

"Where?" Hagan asked as he got up off the bathroom floor and dusted off his hands.

"The dresser," Ryan led the way into the bedroom, "She helped me move it in." Ryan went to the side closest to the bed. Hagan went to the other side.

"Lift from the bottom and only the bottom," Ryan said.

"Okay," Hagan said as he crouched down with Ryan. They both put their hands under the bottom and moved it out from the wall. Once there was enough room for Hagan to work, they put the dresser down. Hagan looked at the backside of the dresser, which had been varnished along with the rest of it. He found the perfect handprint on his side.

"Hers, or yours?" Hagan asked pointing to the print.

"Hers," Ryan said, "I lifted this side and she lifted that one."

"Wonderful," Hagan said as he started dusting the print. When he was finished, he went back for his kit to get a lift for the print. It was a full palm print and as perfect as it could be. Hagan carefully put it away before examining the dresser carefully. He found some strands of hair from where Abigail had gotten hers caught in the edge and had to pull herself free. He looked happy as he squeezed them and put them in a baggie before labelling it.

"That is perfect," Hagan said, "I wish more people moved furniture is such a way."

"You're welcome," Ryan said, "Anything else you need?"

"Not at the moment," Hagan said, "Unless there this place has a security camera."

"The building next door has security cameras on the outside of the building," Ryan said, "But this one doesn't have any."

"I'll have to go talk to them about their cameras," Hagan said as he packed up, "I'll talk to Savanna in the next couple hours and get stuff from her. Perhaps tomorrow, I'll have more information for you."

"Okay," Ryan said as he followed Hagan out to the kitchen. Hagan packed everything into his backpack.

"I'll also see if I can get my computer guy to check your computer over for any monitoring stuff," Hagan said, "If they are monitoring anything then we would have a chance to trace it back to them."

"They don't actually seem too concerned about me," Ryan said.

"But they might become more concerned as I dig

into things," Hagan said, "I already have protection against bugs and stuff. We need to make sure that you are too."

"Fine," Ryan said.

Hagan had everything packed and Ryan showed him out. Once Hagan was gone, Ryan locked the door and went back to his work. Everyone had responded to his e-mails and he had a lot of work to get started.

The next morning, Ryan had finished reviewing the information for the first job when there was a knock at the door. Ryan went to the door and looked out. Hagan was standing in there looking the same as yesterday. Ryan opened the door.

"Morning," Hagan said as he stepped inside the apartment.

"Did you find anything?" Ryan asked as he closed the door.

"She doesn't have a criminal record," Hagan answered, "I'm still waiting on some more information from some of my sources to get back to me. My computer guy couldn't come today, but he gave me a disc that you can install to monitor it from his system. He promises that all your information is safe. If he did anything else, he wouldn't work again."

Ryan and Hagan went into the kitchen. Hagan sat down on the stool before digging in his backpack. He took out the disc and put it on the counter in front of Ryan.

"Did you find anything else?" Ryan asked.

"There was nothing suspicious in your phone records," Hagan answered, "Savanna's cell had nothing on it, so they must have been tracking it through the

GPS. They didn't hack into it, so there was no trace to follow. I have traced Abigail's cell to Flint and I should have access to the records later today. I tried calling the number from a payphone and got the same disconnection message that Savanna did. I then parked myself a short distance away, but within sight of the phone. After half an hour, I thought no one would show up, but then I noticed the car that had pulled to the curb on the other side of the street that had tinted windows. I wrote down the licence plate number, but my sources haven't gotten back to me on that either. No one got out of the car, but it sat there a long while before driving off. That particular phone booth doesn't have a security camera on it, so they don't have my image in their system."

"Speaking of security cameras, did you get the footage from the camera next door?" Ryan asked.

"Yes," Hagan answered, "But I have to do more work on it. The video shows five men in black outfits and masks leaving the building and getting into a van. They have several packages with them. One of the packages is big enough to be a person. What are Abigail's approximate height and weight?"

"Five feet six inches a hundred and fifteen," Ryan said, "Need the rest of the description?"

"Got most of from her friends," Hagan said, "But they weren't sure on height and weight."

"She had let her hair go back to its natural brown," Ryan said.

"I thought her hair was naturally blonde," Hagan said, "That was what everyone else seemed to think as well."

"I thought so too when I first met her, but within a

month it started to change to brown." Ryan said, "I asked her about it and she said she decided to stop dying it."

"That is good to know," Hagan said, "Anything else that you think might help?"

"Abby was smart," Tony said, "But it wasn't like she tried to be smarter than everyone, or make everyone else feel dumb. She could just answer questions that were difficult for anyone else. She was good at mathematics and science with a better grasp of history than I remember ever having. I never asked her where she learned it all, but sometimes I wondered why she didn't use any of it to get a job. Mathematics and science aren't my strong suit; I'm very much the business end of things. Things could be much different when it comes to science things."

"That might help, or it might not," Hagan said, "As I said, I'm waiting for my sources to get back to me. And I have some work to do myself. Install the disc and that piece will be dealt with. And I'll be back tomorrow with hopefully more news." Hagan got to his feet.

"I was going to ask you to check if my phone is tapped," Ryan said.

"Pick it up and listen," Hagan said. Ryan picked up the cordless and pressed the talk button. The dial tone cam on, but he didn't hear anything else.

"What do you hear?" Hagan asked.

"The dial tone," Ryan answered.

"Was there some crackling before the dial tone?" Hagan asked.

"I didn't hear any," Ryan said as he put the cordless on its base.

"Then it isn't tapped," Hagan said, "But listen for

the crackling before you make any phone calls about this case. The deeper I look into it the more dangerous it may get."

"If the men in suits show up here, I'm going to start asking them questions," Ryan said.

"If they let you," Hagan said, "They are very much into making people disappear."

"I have clients that will come looking for me if I don't get back to them within a certain amount of time," Ryan said, "I have at least one that will hound the police until I found, either dead or alive. I'm not worried about disappearing."

"You're braver than I am," Hagan said before leaving the kitchen. Ryan followed him so that he could lock the door once Hagan had left. Ryan took the disc from the kitchen counter into his study. He backed up all his information before installing the program. It only took a few minutes before it was finished.

Ryan went back to work for a few hours before taking a break for lunch. When he finished eating, Ryan went into the living room and looked out the front window to see if the world was still wet. He was surprised to find the rain had stopped and the sun was shining through gaps in the clouds. The sunbeams highlighted parts of the street, like the man standing behind the bench for the bus stop across the street from Ryan's apartment. The man was wearing a dark suit that included a black tie. It was hard to tell from the distance, but it looked like the man had an earpiece. His lips also moved occasionally as if he was talking to an unseen person. The man kept glancing at the apartment, but with the lights off it was unlikely that the man could see Ryan.

Ryan turned from the window and went to the hall closet. He pulled on shoes and coat before grabbing his keys on the way out of the apartment. He went down the steps and onto the street. The man was still standing there across the street, but this time he saw Ryan. He didn't move. Ryan started across the street toward him, but Ryan had to stop and wait for a bus to go passed before he could get to the other curb. The man had disappeared by the time Ryan got there. Ryan looked around, but no sign of the man.

Ryan cursed under his breath before going back across the street. He was just about to the steps when he saw Tony coming down the street. Ryan waited for him.

"Coming or going?" Tony asked.

"Going back inside," Ryan answered.

"Mind if I come up for a little while?" Tony asked.

"For a little while," Ryan said. He started up the stairs and Tony followed.

Inside Ryan led the way to the living room and took the chair by the window. Tony sat down on the couch. He didn't reach for the remote or the TV guide sitting on the coffee table.

"I owe you an explanation," Tony said, "But I would rather it didn't go any farther than this room."

"I don't gossip," Ryan said, "You know that."

"I know," Tony said, "But this is more personal than usual."

"So, what caused this depression?" Ryan asked.

"A little over a year ago, Audrey started to feel sick," Tony said, "She went to the doctor and came back with the great news that she was pregnant. I wanted to shout it to the world, but she made me promise not to tell anyone until three months were up. She even marked the date on the calendar for me. That date seemed to be coming fast and I was getting excited when Audrey was in trouble and I had to take her to the hospital. She had a miscarriage due to a blood type difference or something like that. I didn't completely understand it, but it comes down to Audrey and I have different blood types. I was crushed and she was doing worse. We held on to each other for the first while as we sorted things out. The doctor said that mourning was usual and we would slowly get over it. She got her health back and we picked ourselves up. We avoided too many people and any social situation where we would have to explain what was going on.

"Audrey started looking into whatever happened with the blood types and talked to the doctor several more times. And there is a good chance that it would happen again if she got pregnant again. There are supposed to be medications to help with the matter, but we couldn't figure out if either plan covers them. So, she is worried about getting pregnant again and what could happen, which means that if I so much as try to suggest fooling around, she gets uptight and angry at me. Then I get kicked out and frustrated. And it takes a while to talk her into letting me back in.

"I have no idea what to do about it and she isn't helpful there either. Even when we are together, she doesn't want to talk about it. After she kicks me out, we don't speak at all until I go back to her to beg to be let back in."

"Why don't you find a therapist to talk to?" Ryan asked, "A therapist can help you figure out your head and likely help you figure out what to say to Audrey."

"And where do I find one of those?" Tony asked.

"Try the clinic down the street," Ryan answered, "They should be able to refer to a therapist. It should all be paid for through your work.

"I could try it," Tony said.

"As long as you put some work into it, you should get something back out of it," Ryan said, "Neal went to a therapist after his latest break up and it helped him a lot."

"If it helped Neal then it might help," Tony said, "At this point, anything except what we're currently doing has got to be better."

"That is usually a sign that you are ready for help," Ryan said.

"Why is it that you always seem to know what to for problems?" Tony asked.

"I'm a consultant," Ryan answered, "It is my job to solve other people's problems for them."

"Do I owe any money for this visit?" Tony asked.

"No," Ryan answered, "The only way you would owe money is if I'm solving problems with a company. Personal problems aren't part of my business."

"Thanks for listening anyway," Tony said as he got to his feet.

"Not a problem," Ryan said, "See you later."

"See you," Tony said before leaving the apartment. Ryan turned back to the window and looked out. The man in the suit hadn't returned. Ryan looked to see if he had moved to somewhere else, but didn't see him. Ryan did see Tony headed down the street towards the clinic. Ryan hoped that Tony would find the help he needed.

After making sure that the man in the suit didn't appear to be coming back, Ryan went back to work.

Ryan was about to start supper when the phone rang. He picked it up, "Hello?"

"Wanna come to another performance?" Jey's voice came over the phone.

"Where's tonight's performance?" Ryan asked.

"The usual place," Jey answered, "We've been booked for five nights before we head off to record an album."

"You got the contract?" Ryan asked.

"Yup," Jey answered, "Even paid for to be reviewed by a lawyer to make sure of everything was legit. Should be great. But Savanna suggested that you might need a place to forget your problems."

"I can come to the performance," Ryan said, "Regular start time?"

"Yup," Jey answered.

"See you there," Ryan said.

"Okay," Jey said before hanging up. Ryan put the receiver down. Instead of making supper, he gathered his keys, wallet, and coat.

Ryan stopped for a quick supper before heading for the bar where the group usually played. The bouncer let in him without worrying about the cover charge. The bar wasn't too busy yet, so Ryan easily got the booth closest to the stage. He ordered a drink when the server stopped by. It was delivered just before the bar's manager came on stage to announce the show's opener. The opener was a band that was drum and bass heavy with a singer who stayed too far away from the microphone. Ryan wasn't sure he could tell what the songs were about, let alone quote any of the lyrics.

The opener had just finished when Savanna slid into

the booth.

"Jey tried to convince the manager that the band needed a better opener," Savanna said, "But the manager said that he didn't have any choice because the owner's nephew was in the band, which means that the music sucks and no one can tell him."

Smash came out on stage and started to play. Jey nodded to Ryan and Savanna and Ryan waved back. They started into what was their signature song. The audience cheered and they joined in with the words.

"The audience is well lubricated with an opener like that," Ryan said.

"As long as they don't get too rowdy," Savanna said, "How is the search for Abby?"

"Abigail Ward is a fake identity," Ryan said, "Which doesn't help much in trying to figure out who would kidnap her. Hagan did get footage that she was kidnapped from the camera next door."

"And the men in suits?" Savanna asked.

"Hagan hasn't found much on them yet," Ryan answered, "But I've seen them watching my apartment from across the street. When I went out to confront the man he disappeared. Have you seen any more of them?"

"Not since the mall," Savanna said, "But it must be serious if Abby was kidnapped by men who look like they are government agents."

"I'm trying to figure out why the men in suits are following us around," Ryan said, "They stand out against any background, so we do notice them. We have barely started looking into her disappearance. If they were smart, they would blend in, follow us discretely, and ignore the whole thing until we were a lot closer."

"Maybe they're trying to scare us off," Savanna said, "If we are scared then we'll give up the whole thing and they wouldn't have to worry about us finding anything out."

"Then they are doing a poor job at it," Ryan said, "Having a guy in a suit watching me is hardly scary. I got over any fear of suits on my first consulting job when the owner insisted on standing over my shoulder the whole time."

"I don't know," Savanna said, "Having those guys follow me around the mall was pretty freaky."

"Enough to make you want to give up searching for Abby?" Ryan asked.

"No," Savanna answered, "But enough to make me very worried about her until she is found."

"Then the men in suits aren't working in scaring us away," Ryan said.

"But they don't know that," Savanna said, "They could still think that."

"I went after the man in a suit that I saw today," Ryan said, "I think they'll figure it out fairly quickly."

"What would you have done is you caught him?" Savanna asked.

"Ask him what he thought he was doing," Ryan said, "And where Abby is."

"Do you think he'll answer?" Savanna asked.

"No," Ryan said, "I don't think he'll tell me anything."

The server brought Ryan a refill and took Savanna's order. They didn't talk again, choosing instead to listen to the music.

When the band took a ten-minute break, Savanna

went backstage. Ryan stayed where he was and listened to the generic mix of songs being played. He felt like someone was watching him. Maybe he was getting paranoid with everything going on with the search for Abby.

Savanna came out and sat down as the generic music turned off. The band came back out on stage. They got organized and then started playing to the cheers of the audience. The server brought another round of drinks for Ryan and Savanna. They didn't talk as they sat and enjoyed the music.

About three songs in, Ryan noticed Savanna glancing out into the audience. Her nervous habit of clasping her hands started. Her profile had stiffened up. Ryan leaned closer to her.

"Whoever it is, they aren't going to do anything here," Ryan said.

"How do you know?" Savanna asked.

"They haven't done anything yet," Ryan answered, "Probably too many people who would be witnesses. If they are suddenly interested in actually doing something to us, they will wait until we leave."

"That is only a small comfort," Savanna said.

"The point is, relax," Ryan said, "Nothing is going to happen during the show." Ryan leaned back before taking a sip of his drink. Savanna didn't relax, but she quit trying to find the person in the audience.

When the show was over, Ryan and Savanna stayed in the booth. Most of the audience paid their tab and left. A few people kept drinking. After the rush to leave, the server brought Ryan and Savanna refills. They waited twenty minutes longer before Jey and the keyboardist joined them.

"What did you think of the show?" Jey asked.

"It was great," Ryan answered, "I hadn't heard that one song before. Is it actually new, or have I not been paying enough attention?"

"It's new," the keyboardist said, "We wrote it the other day and was wondering how it would turn out. The audience seemed to love it."

"Or they were too drunk to notice that it was new," Jey said, "We should'a done it earlier in the show."

"I thought it sounded good," Ryan said.

"Hopefully, it'll catch on," Jey said, "Otherwise we're goin' to have a really short career as a band."

"You'll make it," Ryan said, "You already have fans to support you."

"It's the rest of the world that we need to get on our side," the keyboardist said.

"We'll worry about that later," Jey said, "Tonight is for this gig and relaxing. Which calls for another round for everyone." Jey signalled for the server to bring more drinks.

When the bar closed for the night, everyone was kicked out. The rest of the band had taken the instruments after the gig ended, so they were long gone. Ryan, Jey, Savanna, and the keyboardist staggered out of the bar with the bouncer laughing as they supported each other and laughing. They headed down the street.

"Should we have had a cab called?" the keyboardist asked.

"I don't have any cash on me," Jey answered, "Better off calling Oscar."

"Oscar doesn't like picking us up when we're drunk," the keyboardist said, "Especially after that time we made him stop at every gas station between the bar and the house."

"That really pissed him off," Jey chuckled, "The look on his face after the second time we stopped was priceless. He figured that we were up to something, but as long as we weren't robbing the places he wasn't worried. And then we had him stop at each gas station right next to each other."

"The gas station attendants were just as confused when we went in and cleared out their supply of tinned mints," the keyboardist said.

"And Oscar's face the next morning when he found mints in every place we could stuff them in his car," Jey laughed, "He threatened to never let us into his car ever again."

The group reached the corner and stopped.

"I hate to be the downer," the keyboardist said, "But I think we have a shadow." Everyone sobered up a bit as Jey and Savanna checked behind them. They couldn't see anyone, but got the sense of someone back there.

"Suspected as much," Ryan said, "Someone has been watching the table all evening, why wouldn't they follow us?"

"Do you know who?" Jey asked.

"Either someone with criminal intent, or someone related to the men in suits that have been seen around," Ryan answered.

"Doesn't sound good either way," the keyboardist said, "Should we call a cab for here?"

"Doesn't have any money," Jey said.

"My place is closest," Ryan said, "We'll head there and then you guys can get a ride from there."

"What about you?" the keyboardist asked.

"They already know where I live," Ryan answered, "They have it under surveillance. If it is someone if criminal intent, it would be a refreshing change to things."

"You need help," the keyboardist said as they crossed the street toward Ryan's Place.

"It's been a strange couple days," Ryan said.

"I wonder what the attendant of that last gas station thought when he found all those mint tins in the bathroom garbage," Jey said.

"I bet he checked the mint stock," the keyboardist said before both burst out laughing.

The gas stations incident and the laughter associated lasted the rest of the way to Ryan's apartment. They were just about to go up the stairs when Ryan saw something lying on the bench under the porch beside the stairs. He looked again and realized that it was a person lying there. Ryan went over to see who it was. It was Tony wrapped in his jacket with his eyes closed.

"Tony," Ryan shook his shoulder. Tony opened his eyes and looked up at Ryan.

"Sorry," Tony said as he sat up, "I was looking for a place to crash and I didn't realize you weren't home and I couldn't find anywhere else to go."

"Come inside," Ryan said before going back to where everyone else was waiting. Tony got up and followed them up the stairs.

Ryan unlocked the door and let everyone in. They removed their shoes before finding places to slouch on the furniture, but no one was in a rush to turn on the lights. Ryan went into the kitchen and got the cordless. He brought it back to the living room and offered it to Jey. Jey took it. Ryan went to the window and looked out. He saw a man standing in the shadows of the building across the street, but he couldn't see any details. He couldn't tell if it was the man in the suit from earlier, or someone new. Ryan pulled the curtain closed before turning on the table lamp. Tony was already asleep in the chair. The keyboardist was half asleep in the other chair. Savanna had fallen asleep leaning against Jey, who was staring at the phone as if he wasn't sure what it was.

Ryan took the cordless before turning the lamp off. He put the phone back in the kitchen before crawling fully clothed into his bed. Ryan let his eyes close.

CHAPTER THREE

The phone rang, causing Ryan to sit up and open his eyes. His head started to ache the minute it realized he was awake. The phone rang again and vibrated in Ryan's head. He put his hands over his ears and closed his eyes against the pain. The phone rang demanding an answer for the third time, but Ryan didn't really want to talk to anyone at the moment. The fourth ring was muffled by his hands but still vibrated in his head. There was no fifth ring. Ryan took his hands from over his ears and looked at the phone. He stared at it for a full minute before he heard movement out in the living room.

Ryan wanted to try and go back to sleep, but the memory of his guests in the living room came back to him. He wondered if one of them had gotten the phone, or whether the person calling gave up after five rings. Ryan got out of bed and changed clothes into some that were clean. Then he went out to the kitchen. Tony was sitting on the stool eating a sandwich.

"Sorry about crashing here," Tony said.

"Yeah, whatever," Ryan said as he poured himself a glass of water. He used it to wash down some painkillers.

"This is what you fourth hangover in a week," Tony said.

"Doesn't really matter," Ryan said, "There isn't much else for me to do at the moment."

"Don't you have work to do?" Tony asked.

"Done some of that too," Ryan answered, "But it gets lonely in the evenings. Fortunately, I haven't been drinking alone."

"I noticed," Tony pointed a thumb towards the living room where there were some groans.

"Did you get the phone?" Ryan asked.

"No," Tony answered, "I would have if you hadn't gotten it on that last ring, but then it stopped. Unless I'm confused and you picked it up."

"I didn't pick it up," Ryan said. The keyboardist stumbled into the kitchen and sat down on the other stool.

"Painkillers?" Ryan offered him the bottle.

"Why not," the keyboardist said taking the bottle. He shook some into his hand and swallowed them without any water.

"Makes me glad I wasn't out drinking," Tony said.

"You have money to drink?" Ryan asked.

"No," Tony answered, "But at the moment, I'm not missing the hangover."

"Do you usually have someone phoning so early in the morning?" the keyboardist asked.

"No," Ryan answered, "But they didn't stay on the

line long enough to figure out who it was, or why they were calling."

"Well, nothing is going to wake the other two before noon," the keyboardist said, "Did Jey call Oscar?"

"I don't remember him doing so," Ryan answered.

"Probably didn't figure out who was following us either," the keyboardist said.

"Nope," Ryan said.

"Should call Oscar and let him know where we are," the keyboardist said. Ryan reached for the phone and it rang. Ryan picked it up and pressed the talk button.

"Hello?"

"Ryan? This is Oscar," the voice on the other end said, "Have you seen half the band and a girlfriend?"

"Yup," Ryan answered, "A quarter of it was just about to call you and let you know where they were. Would you like to speak with him?"

"Yes," Oscar said.

"Here you go," Ryan said before offering the phone to the keyboardist. The keyboardist took the phone.

"Yes, Oscar, we fell asleep at Ryan's place. The other two are still asleep and probably won't be awake for a few more hours. I would still be asleep, but a phone call a few minutes ago woke me up. Really? I'm sure that Ryan is appreciative as I am for that. Good for him, but the other two aren't going anywhere until after noon. Good luck with that. You can come pick us up after noon. Bye." The keyboardist handed the phone back to Ryan, who put it back on its base.

"Oscar was the person who phoned earlier," the keyboardist said, "He hung up after five rings because he thought you might be sleeping and would have picked up the phone otherwise. He phoned back because our new manager told him to. The manager wants us all to meet up for breakfast. I figured that Oscar can explain that the band doesn't eat breakfast after one of our gigs."

"You're not worried about his dumping you?" Tony asked.

"We just signed a contract with him," the keyboardist answered, "Nowhere on it did it specify that we needed to be available for breakfast. If he wants breakfast, he can eat alone. Oscar had gotten a hold of Chase and Adam already. They said the same thing I did. Apparently, they went home before starting to drink, but they are hungover as well."

"Your new manager might have to enjoy Oscar's company for breakfast," Ryan said.

"Oscar won't eat breakfast with him," the keyboardist said, "He had his breakfast a lot earlier in the day because he gets up early to work out. Oscar likes to eat before he works out."

"That will be one quiet breakfast," Tony said. The keyboardist laughed before wincing in pain.

"You have until noon," Ryan said, "to see if you can get some sleep."

"I might try that," the keyboardist said as he got up. He went back into the living room.

"What about you?" Tony asked.

"I might as well see if I can get some work done," Ryan answered as he picked his glass of water, "I'm already in pain anyway." Ryan headed for his study.

Half an hour later, there was a knock on the study door. Ryan looked up to see Tony standing there.

"Yes?" Ryan asked.

"I was wondering if I could crash on your couch for

a few days longer," Tony said.

"Did you find a counsellor?" Ryan asked.

"And have an appointment every day at one in the afternoon," Tony answered.

"Then you can stay for a little while," Ryan said.

"Thank you," Tony said before leaving. Ryan turned back to his work.

About noon Ryan could hear more people talking and moving around, so he went out to the kitchen. Tony was making himself lunch. The keyboardist was looking far more rested as he drank some water. Jey and Savanna were making use of the bottle of painkillers Ryan had left on the counter.

"You didn't go back to sleep?" the keyboardist asked.

"No, I figured I would get some work done," Ryan said, "Since I have nothing up this evening I should be able to enjoy a full night's sleep. That will make up for not going back to sleep this morning."

"You don't want to come to the gig tonight, then," Jey said.

"As much as I enjoy your gigs, I think I need a break to get some sleep," Ryan said.

"We aren't insulted," Jey said, "You have been one of our biggest supporters over the years and we know that you will come to other gigs."

"You'll have lots of fun without me," Ryan said.

"Did you find out who followed us?" Jey asked.

"No," Ryan answered, "I looked out the window when we got back, but he was in the shadows and I couldn't see any details to tell who it was."

"Did they come back?" Jey asked.

"I haven't checked out there today," Ryan said,

"Though I probably should. I'll be right back." Ryan went into the living room and looked out the window. He didn't see anyone that looked suspicious, or men in suits. But Oscar's car was pulling up to the curb. Ryan went back to the kitchen.

"Your ride is here," Ryan said.

"Then we better get out of here," the keyboardist said as he stood up.

"Come on," Jey nudged Savanna. She slowly got to her feet as he did. They followed the keyboardist into the entryway. Ryan followed them.

"Thank you for letting us crash here," the keyboardist said.

"Not a problem," Ryan said.

"See you again," Jey said.

"Have fun at your gig," Ryan said.

"Will do," Jey said.

The keyboardist opened the door and the three of them left. Ryan closed the door before going into the living room. One of the other band members had stepped out of the car, but that was as far as he had gotten before the others came into view. All of them got into the car before it pulled away. Ryan watched until it turned the corner at the end of the street and then he looked over the street. There was still nothing suspicious that he could identify.

Ryan went back to the kitchen where Tony was just sitting down to eat lunch. Tony looked up at Ryan.

"Did you want some?" Tony asked.

"No," Ryan answered. He started making himself a sandwich.

Ryan was just about to finish putting the sandwich together when there was a knock on the door.

"Expecting someone?" Tony asked.

"Sort of," Ryan answered before going to the door. He looked through the eyehole to see Hagan standing there. Ryan opened the door and let Hagan in. After closing the door, Ryan led the way into the kitchen. Hagan sat down on the other stool and put his bag on the counter. Tony and Hagan studied each other, trying to figure out what to think of each other.

"Hagan, this is Tony," Ryan said, "He's a friend who is currently crashing on my couch. Tony, this is Hagan. He's a private investigator I hired to look into Abby's disappearance."

"Disappearance?" Tony looked surprised, "I thought she just took off." Hagan looked like he had decided that Tony was okay.

"Except that she missed a prearranged shopping trip with Savanna," Ryan said, "And if you phone her cell men in suits show up to follow you around."

"That's weird," Tony said.

"Hence me," Hagan said.

"Does this have anything to do with you and the rest being followed back from the gig last night?" Tony asked.

"Without having seen the person, I don't know," Ryan answered, "But it seems likely. There was a man in a suit out there yesterday, but he disappeared when I went across the street to confront him."

"So, I should be careful of anyone following me," Tony said.

"Probably," Ryan said.

"I haven't found much for connection to the men in suits," Hagan said, "But I expect that to be buried deep."

"What have you found?" Ryan asked.

"I finished the search on her DNA and fingerprints," Hagan said, "As I said before she has no criminal record, but after some searching I found a missing person report. The person reported missing is a Selena Stafferson, who at the time was a fourteen-year-old foster child. She was reported missing by her seventeen-year-old brother Russell, who was also a foster child. The officer listened to Russell, filed a report that included fingerprints and DNA, and then spoke to the foster parents. The foster parents claimed she hadn't disappeared, but had been moved to a home better suited for her needs. The school administrators backed up the foster parents and said that she had been moved to a school for smart children. So the officer left the file open, but didn't look deeper into the case."

"What happened to the brother?" Ryan asked.

"Russell Stafferson finished high school, moved out of the group home, went to university, got a degree in engineering, and now lives with his wife in his hometown." Hagan answered, "When I tried to phone him, he hung up on me and then screened my calls. I think he might be more willing to talk on a face to face basis, but I don't know for sure."

"Do you have his address?" Ryan asked.

"Yes," Hagan said. He dug in his backpack and pulled out a piece of paper. He placed it on the counter for Ryan.

"Did you find out anything else about her past?" Ryan asked as he took the paper and tucked it into his pocket.

"I'm still looking into getting her school records," Hagan answered, "I'm also looking into the foster parents, but I'm having a little bit of trouble finding their names. Since I don't have her records from being in government care, I don't have any of the information. I'm working on getting those."

"And her cellphone?" Ryan asked.

"I got the records," Hagan answered, "But most of them were calls to friends and there is no way to tell how the men in suits are tracing people who are calling her cell."

"You used the word most," Ryan said.

"There are three calls that I'm still working on," Hagan said, "They were from unlisted numbers to her cell and any information is hard to find. However, all three calls were made to her cell within the first two years of her owning it."

"But she didn't call them?" Ryan asked.

"No trace of it," Hagan answered, "All three conversations lasted five minutes exactly, so she knew the person. And it isn't Flint's number. She must have given someone else the phone number. As I said I'm working on figuring who is was. The last thing I have for you is the security video from the building next door." Hagan pulled a laptop out of his bag and set it up on the counter. Ryan moved around so that he could see the screen. The laptop was turned on, so Hagan went right into the program.

A video came up on the screen. It showed the street out front of Ryan's apartment as seen from the side of the building next door. It was night, so the street lights were the only thing casting light on the scene, but it was pretty easy to see what was going on. It looked like a fairly normal night with all the usual cars parked in their spaces and no signs of people. Then a dark coloured cargo van comes down the street. It parks in from of Ryan's apartment. Nothing happened for several minutes and then the door opened. Four people in dark clothing with bags came out and disappeared out of frame toward the apartment.

Hagan fast-forwarded through fifteen minutes of video and then let it play again. The four men came back into the frame with their bags, except the last man had an extra bag slung over one shoulder that looked like a body bag with a body inside it. They helped him carefully put the body bag inside the van before they all climbed back in. The door was shut and the van pulled away.

"Now, I understand why you hired someone to investigate Abby's disappearance," Tony said.

"As you can see, they were fast, effective, and knew exactly what they were doing," Hagan said, "The van has no license plate, so I can't trace it that way. The computer has scanned it for any characteristics that could identify it and found none. It looks like any other cargo van. Based on the height and weight the scanner program told me, they are male and in good shape. Based on their outfits I would guess military, but which branch I can't tell."

"They can't be mercenaries hired to do this?" Tony asked.

"They could be, but with the way they move they have spent time in the military," Hagan answered, "And since none of them show any signs of shrugging off the military type movement, they are either still in the military or fresh out. If they are fresh out then it must be the whole squad that went mercenary. However, with the men in black suits following people around, I would go with military. Most mercenaries wouldn't bother to follow people around, or chase after ghost calls. A private company would hire professionals to follow people around rather than men in black suits, who stand out in just about any setting. After all, they hired professionals for the kidnapping part."

"That makes sense," Tony said, "If she has been kidnapped, why are they monitoring her cellphone?"

"I'm assuming government paranoia," Hagan answered, "Or stupidity. That is another reason that I suspect the military. The kidnapping was pulled off to perfection, with no one being the wiser about her disappearance. Even Savanna might not have been the wiser, though sad or upset about the missed shopping. The men following people who call her cellphone is more of something from top paranoids would think up, which would be why the men in black suits show up. All this adds up to a lot of work for me, as I try to dig into what the military wanted with Abby and why other government branches would want to cover it up."

"Don't get into trouble over this," Ryan said, "I don't want you to get arrested, or anything."

"The case is fun for that reason, but I won't get in trouble if I am careful," Hagan said, "I wouldn't have it any other way."

"Okay," Ryan said.

"So, that is all that I have at the moment," Hagan said, "Were you thinking of going to talk to Russell?"

"Yes," Ryan answered, "I'll have to see what there is for flights available."

"I'll see what I can dig up while you are gone," Hagan said, "If you find any information that would be helpful, let me know when you get back. It is not currently a good idea to call me, so wait until I come over."

"Okay," Ryan said.

Hagan packed up his laptop and put it back in his bag. When he finished, he got to his feet. Ryan followed him to the entryway. Hagan opened the door and stepped outside. Ryan closed the door behind him before going back to the kitchen.

"So, you are leaving?" Tony asked, "Does that mean I have to find somewhere else to stay?"

"Yes, I'm leaving," Ryan answered, "You can stay here and keep my apartment safe and bug free."

"Insect infestation?" Tony asked.

"Computerized bugs," Ryan answered.

"Yeah, okay," Tony said.

Ryan finished making his sandwich before taking it to the study. Ryan looked up ticket prices and found a flight that left this evening. He bought the ticket and printed it off. Then he went back to work.

About suppertime, Ryan went out to the kitchen. Tony was in the living room watching TV. Ryan made himself a sandwich. Then he packed an overnight bag. Ryan called a cab, left the key with Tony, double-checked that he had everything, and then met the cab at the curb.

The flight was on time. Ryan was able to put in earplugs and sleep through the flight.

The plane landed about eight in the morning. Ryan stopped for breakfast at the airport coffee shop before finding a cab. The cab dropped him off across the street from the address Hagan had given him. Once the cab was gone, Ryan looked at the house. It was white with navy trim, a fence around the yard, climbing toys scattered in the front yard, a black SUV in front of the garage, and a path from the gate to the door. There was a light on inside and some movement.

The rest of the neighbourhood looked similar with quiet houses and toys in the yard. No one seemed to have noticed his arrival and no one was watching out windows. Someone at the far end of the street was getting into their car.

Ryan crossed the street, through the open gate, and up the walk to the door. He rang the doorbell and waited. A few minutes went past before the door opened. The man who stood there was a little taller than Ryan, a regular build, wearing blues jeans and a t-shirt with bare feet. His facial features, brown eyes, and brown hair all reminded Ryan of Abby and he had no doubt that they were siblings.

"Is there something I can help you with?" Russell asked.

"I am looking for Selena Stafferson and I was hoping you could help," Ryan answered.

"She has been missing a long time," Russell crossed his arms over his chest and leaned on the door jam, "Why are so many people interested now?"

"Because she showed up six months ago," Ryan answered, "And then she was kidnapped a couple days ago. The thought was that perhaps her first disappearance can help figured out what happened this time."

"And your relationship to Selena?" Russell asked.

"I met her at a concert six months ago and she has been living with me ever since," Ryan answered.

"You weren't the one who called," Russell said.

"No, that was Hagan," Ryan said, "He is the private investigator I hired to help look for her."

"I'm not sure what I can tell," Russell said as he dropped his arms to his sides and stepped out of the way. Ryan entered the house and Russell closed the door. Ryan slipped off his shoes before following Russell down the hallway to the kitchen. The hallway went all the way through the house and at the end was a mudroom with the back door. The walls were cream, the table was a dark wood with a mirror over it, a staircase went up on the right side, and there were two doorways on the left side. The closest looked to go into a living room and the second was the kitchen.

"Coffee?" Russell asked.

"Sure," Ryan answered as he sat down at the kitchen table. Russell poured Ryan a cup of coffee and brought it to the table along with a mug that was already sitting on the counter.

"I haven't seen Selena since she was fourteen," Russell said, "She had been living with a foster family, while I was in a group home. We saw each other at school and occasionally, we would spend some time together after school. Most people think that we wouldn't want to spend time because we were siblings, but we were all we had. Our parents had died three years before and it had been hard on both of us. Most people didn't understand what we had gone through so it was harder to talk to them than each other.

"She hadn't been at school for a couple of days and her foster parents refused to tell me anything because I wasn't eighteen and I wasn't her legal guardian. Then she didn't show up to our arranged time, and she always managed to make it even if she had to sneak out.

The only time she couldn't make it, she had let me know. So, I went to the police officer who came around to the school and gave us lectures on trusting the police. He took down the information, gathered stuff to identify her if she was ever found, and promised to look into it.

"He came back to me after three days and told me what he had been told. According to both the school and her foster parents, Selena had been sent to a school for super-smart students. He had tried to get some paperwork to prove it, but neither the school nor her foster parents were willing to provide it. He seemed suspicious of the foster parents. He told me that Selena hadn't taken any of her belongings with her. Instead, her foster parents had just thrown it out and he had collected it from the trash. He let me pick through it for anything sentimental. The officer also promised me that he would keep looking when he could spare the time, but because her foster parents had given a statement about where she was his supervisor assumed that the case was closed.

"I haven't heard anything about Selena since then and I haven't heard anything from the officer either. When I was eighteen, I had tried again to get information about her. I was able to get the court to identify me as her legal guardian, so I could get information from the school and social services. The school gave me the letter that the foster parents had given to them. It was from a school for students that are into math and science. It was a formal letter with the school's name and coat of arms. I looked the school up and found that it didn't exist. Social services let me see their file on Selena, but they didn't know what happened to her either. They didn't go searching for her because her worker had too many files and not enough time to check on all of them. I couldn't track down the foster parents to get them to answer any questions and social services didn't know where they were either. According to the records, the foster parents had a change in situation and the children in their care were moved to other foster homes before they moved without leaving a forwarding address.

"I wasn't able to afford a private investigator to look into the matter at the time because I could barely afford to pay my own rent, without worrying about any extra expenses. Then I was busy with university and haven't gotten back to it. My money has been put toward paying off my student debt and living expenses. I found a woman, who I love, and we have two children. Life has been marching on for me and I have limited time to search for her as much as I would like to see her again.

"What have you found about where she was all this time? Did the private investigator find out anything about it? Did she say anything about her history?"

"She didn't talk about her past at all," Ryan answered, "We talked about current events and our shared love of music. The private investigator has turned up information about her fake identity, which goes back seven years. The name was Abigail Ward and it was made for her. She refused to give the man her name and only went by the one he gave her. They were introduced by a bartender, who didn't know her name either. From there, she drifted around until six months ago when I met her. Hagan, the private investigator, traced her to the missing persons report by DNA and fingerprints. We also have video of her being removed from my apartment by several men. My apartment had also been cleaned of her during that time. We haven't figure out where she is now and we were hoping that figuring out her past might help us figure that out."

"You find that school and you might find out where she was," Russell said, "Her former foster parents might help with that, if you can track them down."

"Do you still have the letter about the school, or any other records that could help?" Ryan asked.

"Yes," Russell answered, "I can get you copies."

"That would be very helpful," Ryan said, "Hopefully Hagan can use them to track down the school and where she went. From there, we'll have to figure out if it has anything to do with where she is now."

"If you wait here, I'll get copies for her," Russell said.

"Okay," Ryan said. Russell got up and left the kitchen.

Ryan stayed where he was and looked around. The kitchen was the same cream as the hallway. The cabinets matched the dark wood table from the hallway, while the counters and the curtains were dark blue. There were the modern conveniences usually found in a kitchen like the mounted plastic wrap dispenser, the built-in coffee maker, a dishwasher, and hooks for pans. It was spotless, with the only dirty dishes being the two coffee mugs. It hardly looked like children lived here. Since Abby had never bothered with cleanliness, it surprised Ryan that her brother would have such a spotless house.

Russell came back with a file folder. He put it on the table in front of Ryan before sitting down.

"What was Selena like?" Russell asked.

"She liked music," Ryan answered, "Preferably a live show, over any other kind. She also liked the social aspect of it all. If she found herself in a room of strangers, she would have a room of friends before the evening is over and she would be invited back for the next night. She liked shopping, but rarely had enough money to do anything more than look. She was a good listener and great at remembering things, but she didn't talk about herself much. She would rather go out for a walk than watch TV. Sometimes she seemed to have no purpose in life, except to listen to music, because she never seemed to need any work, or projects. However, she found a reason to live each day and enjoyed every minute of it. Very little could get her angry, when something did she was usually mad enough to be violent. I saw her angry about twice and both times I was a safe distance to avoid flying objects. Both episodes were short and both made me want to avoid making her angry with me. She seemed very happy during the time we were together, but she didn't say anything."

"She wasn't much in verbally expressing emotions before she disappeared," Russell said, "After our parents died, she just shut that part of herself off. We both probably should have had grief counselling, but we didn't get anything more than separated and told to get on with life. I tried to get her to talk about her emotions, but she would shut down for me. Before our parents died, she was happy and careful free. After the worries of the world started to creep into her eyes and she kept everything inside. No one else seemed to notice, not even teachers who she had before. But no one listens to a seventeen-year-old, who lives in a group home. She must have worked most of it out though if she is back to being her normal self. I wish I could have seen her."

"If she can be found, maybe she can come visit," Ryan said.

"You can ask her," Russell said, "But if she didn't visit, I'm sure she had a good reason for not coming."

"We never really discussed our family," Ryan said, "So, I don't know."

"If you find her, just tell her that I miss her," Russell said, "And I hope she finds happiness."

"I will," Ryan said as he picked up the file folder, "Thank you for the information."

"I hope it helps," Russell said as they stood up. Ryan and Russell went to the front door, where Ryan pulled on his shoes. Then Russell opened the door.

"Thank you again," Ryan said.

"You're welcome," Russell said. Ryan stepped onto the path and headed toward the gate. He heard the door close behind him. Ryan left the yard through the gate.

Ryan walked the couple blocks to the local convenience store, where they had some tables inside. He bought himself lunch of a sandwich, drink, and small bag of chips. Ryan found a place to sit down and open the file as he started eating. The first sheet inside the folder was an official-looking letter. It was from the Platt Truman School for Exceptional Students and addressed to Mr. and Mrs. Warner. Ryan skipped reading the letter and went right to the person the letter was from; a Mr. Ronald Lathrop with the title of dean the school.

Ryan flipped to the next page. It was the start of an

entry of a social services file. It listed the name Selena Stafferson as the child and Lily Dale as the worker. There was very little in the report sections. It listed the basic facts, like Selena's parents were dead and that she had a brother. She was placed in a foster home with Mr. and Mrs. Warner as foster parents. There was little actual information on either Selena or her foster parents.

This page was stapled to the next one. Ryan flipped it over. It was a copy of a police report on how Selena's parents died. Ryan felt like he should skip the page, but found himself drawn to read it. The account was dry reading and had few details, but the facts were there. It was a carjacking, but they didn't seem to be too interested in the car since the thieves dumped it a few blocks away. As far as anyone could tell, there was nothing else stolen. By the time help arrived it was too late to save them. Selena and Russell were at a babysitter's place for the evening, so they weren't in the car. There were no other facts about the incident or the investigation.

Ryan flipped to the next page and found a school record of grades for Selena Stafferson. She had above-average grades for most of her time at high school. The only time they were down was her first semester. Selena was best in math and science. Everything fit with what Ryan knew or had been told. Ryan turned the page, but there was nothing else in the file. He flipped back to the first page again. It was the letter from the school and he skimmed through it. According to the letter, Selena's grades were good enough that she had been given a test and scored so well that she qualified for the school. The tuition was going to be forgiven because she scored so high and her home situation.

It sounded like any other letter from such a school, except for the lack of explanation about where the money for her schooling would come from. Most of the time there was a scholarship offered, it would be identified in the letter. There was also no mention of what kind of score Selena had gotten or what kind of tests she had been given. Not even which subjects she was so good in. There was so little information about why she was being accepted into the school and the school itself. It triggered some suspicion in Ryan, but he supposed her foster parents would not have questioned it because they had so many other things on their minds.

Ryan closed the file. He put the trash from his lunch in the garbage can before leaving the convenience store. Then Ryan called a cab to pick him up, however, he asked the driver to take him to the address he had for the Warners. It was in a different residential neighbourhood on the other side of town, but a similar economic level. Ryan asked the driver to wait.

The house had a large yard with several pieces of play equipment scattered around it. There were no children visible, but their presence was. The house itself was light blue and a small porch in front of the door. There was no doorbell, just a knocker shaped like a woodpecker. Ryan used it and then waited. It was several minutes before the door opened and a woman stood there. She appeared to be in her mid-fifties or early sixties.

"Yes?" the woman asked.

"I am looking for Liza Warner," Ryan answered.

"I am sorry, but you have the wrong house," the

woman said. The way her eyes shifted Ryan could tell she was lying, but he did not feel he was in a position to call her on it.

"This is 1763 Lyon Street?" Ryan asked.

"Yes, it is," the woman answered, "No one named Liza Warner lives here."

"How long have you lived here?" Ryan asked.

"Six years," the woman answered.

"Then perhaps it was before you moved here," Ryan said, "Do you know the people who lived here before you?"

"I do not," the woman answered, "They had moved long before they sold it and my husband and I bought it through a realtor."

"Is there anyone in the neighbourhood who would remember the Warners?" Ryan asked.

"I don't believe so," the woman answered.

"I am sorry to have bothered you then," Ryan said, "Mrs?"

"Lindsay Wilson," the woman answered, "I am sorry I can't help you."

She started to close the door. Ryan made no attempt to stop her and instead headed back to the street. He got into the waiting cab.

"Are you a former foster child?" the cab driver asked as he got the cab moving.

"No, but my girlfriend is," Ryan answered, "How did you know that is a foster home?"

"Because some of my cousins ended up there," the cab driver answered, "She is nice enough."

"That sounds like she could be better," Ryan said.

"She isn't abusive or anything like that," the cab driver said, "She just prefers white kids."

"That is a problem," Ryan said.

"But not an uncommon problem," the cab driver said, "Especially in the system. Your girlfriend white?"

"As far as I can tell," Ryan answered, "She hasn't told me otherwise."

"Then she was treated better if she was there," the cab driver said.

"The lady who answered the door said it must have been the previous owners who were the foster parents to my girlfriend," Ryan said.

"Not sure why she would say that," the cab driver said, "Her and her husband took a several year break from being foster parents but they have been living there for twenty years or more."

"I wonder why she lied," Ryan said.

"There have been some questionable things happen there," the cab driver said, "That was the reason they stopped taking in foster kids for several years."

"And they keep getting foster kids?" Ryan asked.

"Too many kids, not enough space, and none of it is considered endangering the kids," the cab driver answered.

"I guess that is understandable," Ryan said, "Even if it doesn't seem right."

"Plenty of things don't seem right," the cab driver said, "But they happen anyway."

"True," Ryan said.

The cab driver pulled up to the unloading area at the airport. Ryan paid the fare before collecting his bag and going inside. His flight was not going to be for a couple hours, so he found somewhere to sit. There had been no point trying to do anything else, even if he could. The only other address he had was for the school and it was not in this town. He was not sure he would have been able to find anything there anyway. It might be better for Hagan to look into first.

Before the flight, Ryan found something for supper. Then he got on the flight home. Once again, he used earplugs and slept through the flight.

CHAPTER FOUR

Tony was sitting in the kitchen eating cereal. Ryan set his bag down before sitting across the counter from Tony.

"Get what you were looking for?" Tony asked.

"Mostly," Ryan answered, "But there is a lot more to look into."

"Of course there is," Tony said.

"How goes your therapy?" Ryan asked.

"It is going to take a while," Tony answered, "I have asked Audrey if she would be willing to come, but she isn't ready yet."

"You may have to give her some time," Ryan said.

"That is what the counsellor said," Tony said, "I'm not sure whether Audrey and I will survive this and maybe I should start looking for my own apartment."

"I may have to go out of town again," Ryan said, "So, you can stay on my couch a while longer. I know that isn't the answer to your problems, but it should give you some breathing room for the moment. Any phone calls or other messages?"

"No," Tony answered, "What are your plans now?"

"Work until Hagan stops by," Ryan answered, "I will need the money to pay both Hagan and my bills."

"Need me to contribute while I am here?" Tony asked.

"No," Ryan answered, "I knew I was going to have to take on the work when I asked Hagan to take the case."

"Gonna eat first?" Tony asked.

"I probably should," Ryan answered. He poured himself some cereal and added a little milk before taking the bowl into his office. Ryan ate his breakfast as he got started with his work.

Ryan made a trip to the kitchen when he needed to put the bowl and spoon into the dishwasher. Then he went back to work until lunch. He went back out to the kitchen long enough to make himself a sandwich. Tony had been in the living room when Ryan had brought his bowl out, but was not there when Ryan came out to make his sandwich. Ryan took the sandwich back to his office to keep working.

It was late in the afternoon when Ryan heard a knock at the door. He got up and went to check who it was. He saw Hagan through the peephole and opened the door.

"How was your trip?" Hagan asked as he followed Ryan into the kitchen after Ryan closed the door.

"I got a couple things from her brother," Ryan answered, "Once he was an adult, he managed to get the letter the school was given by her foster parents about what happened to her. He gave me a copy of that."

"That will help," Hagan said as he sat down on the stool. Ryan brought the file and set it in front of Hagan, who flipped it open and scanned the first page.

"I stopped at the address of the foster parents while I was there," Ryan said.

"Did you learn anything from that?" Hagan asked without looking up.

"The lady said she was not the person I was looking for, but I could tell she was lying," Ryan answered, "And the cab driver, who drove me to the airport, confirmed it. Apparently, they took a break from fostering after Abby was sent away and went back to it after some years."

"That sounds suspicious," Hagan said, "I wonder if I can find information about that. It will help now that I have their names."

"The name she gave me when I asked her was Lindsay Wilson," Ryan said.

"Good to know," Hagan said as he made a note of that.

"Have you found anything else?" Ryan asked.

"I am still waiting for someone to get back to me," Hagan answered, "But I should hear from them before the end of the day today. I did get the number that had called her cellphone and I have connected to a man named Guy, but I have not turned up a last name or any other information connected to it."

"Once again, I don't recognize the name," Ryan said, "But that does not surprise me in this case. There are times when I wish we had talked about our histories and others when I only wish she hadn't disappeared."

"It might be best for her not to talk about her

history," Hagan said, "Based on what I've found so far, I probably wouldn't share that history either. When one is running from people, it is easier to not share than chance the wrong person hearing things."

"There is that," Ryan said.

"Did her brother say anything else that might be helpful?" Hagan asked.

"He was the one who reported her missing," Ryan answered, "The cop was suspicious of the foster parents but didn't really get a chance to investigate it because his supervisor figured that the letter to the school was the end of it. But he hadn't heard from her since then and he didn't get much information when he tried to gain it later. He did get himself declared her legal guardian but it didn't help."

"He should have been able to get the information," Hagan said, "So, there must be someone blocking things. That explains some of the issues I have been having with the matter."

"Is it going to be too much trouble?" Ryan asked.

"No, I will do what I can," Hagan answered, "Have you seen any more of those men in suits?"

"I have not," Ryan answered, "But I didn't see any during the trip and I have been in my office all of today. I will keep an eye out."

"What about your friend?" Hagan asked.

"He didn't say anything when I talked to him this morning," Ryan answered, "But I can ask him when he gets back."

"Then I will talk to you tomorrow," Hagan said as he got up. He put the file folder into his bag.

"Okay," Ryan said as he followed Hagan to the door, "I hope more information turns up."

"It should," Hagan said. He left and Ryan closed the door behind him. After locking the door, Ryan went to the living room and looked out the window. He saw Hagan heading down the street. Ryan looked to see if there were any men in suits, but he did not see anyone suspicious. He headed back to his office to get more work done.

Ryan stopped after sending the last e-mail for the job he had been doing to stretch. He heard the door unlock and someone come inside. Ryan got up and went into the kitchen. Tony was the one who had come in and he was carrying a pizza box. He set the box on the counter and got some napkins before sitting down on the stool.

"I'm willing to share if you are tired of sandwiches," Tony said.

"Thanks," Ryan said as he sat down on the other stool. He took a napkin before taking a piece of pizza and setting the piece down on the napkin.

"I spent a couple hours with Audrey," Tony said.

"How did that go?" Ryan asked.

"We didn't talk about our problems and it went well," Tony answered, "It reminds me of how good our relationship was, but then I get sad because it is no longer there."

"That is frustrating," Ryan said before picking up and taking a bite of the pizza.

"Yeah," Tony said, "But she is refusing to talk about any of our problems since I told her I was going to a counsellor. Not that she was much into talking before."

"She is hurting too," Ryan said.

"I know," Tony said, "But if she is not willing to talk about it, I don't know what to do."

"Maybe she isn't ready to talk," Ryan said, "Maybe what you need to do is to sit in silence with her. Maybe you pushing her to talk is not helping her right now. Everyone deals with things differently."

Tony nodded but did not try to say anything around the bite of pizza. They ate without speaking for a couple pieces of pizza.

"Did your PI stop in with more information?" Tony asked.

"He stopped in but didn't have much information for me," Ryan answered, "More like I gave him information rather than the other way around."

"So, what now?" Tony asked.

"Not much until tomorrow," Ryan answered, "Hagan thinks he might have more information then. Until then I will continue to get work done."

"How are you doing with Abby being missing and this search for her?" Tony asked.

"I'm trying not to think about it," Ryan answered.

"Do you think you will actually be able to find her?" Tony asked.

"I don't know," Ryan answered, "I keep hoping, but there is no certainty in the matter."

"Based on what I have seen of Hagan's investigation, Abby had been taken by a military organization," Tony said, "You work as a consultant. How are you going to get her away from them if you find her? Do you have any idea how to do that?"

"No," Ryan answered, "But I will figure it out. I can't leave her there. They kidnapped her, so she doesn't want to be there."

"But what about you?" Tony asked, "These are dangerous people. They could kill you and then what?"

"I will do what I can to survive this," Ryan answered, "I can't help her if I am dead."

"You haven't thought about this," Tony said.

"I haven't," Ryan said, "My concern has been about Abby and I haven't thought about anything else."

"Maybe you should," Tony said, "Because there are plenty of people who don't want to lose you."

"And I should abandon Abby because you won't have a couch to crash on anymore?" Ryan asked.

"That is not what I am saying," Tony said.

"Then what are you saying?" Ryan asked.

"I am worried that you haven't thought this through," Tony answered, "And it isn't just me who would miss you. I am sure Jey and the rest of Smash would be upset if anything happened to you."

"Like much of life, nothing is permanent," Ryan said.

"Doesn't mean it should be thrown away," Tony said.

"I am not throwing anything away," Ryan said, "I am purposely doing something with my life. If Audrey was kidnapped, wouldn't you look for her?"

"I would," Tony said, "But you haven't known Abby for a full year even."

"So, because I haven't known her as long as you have known Audrey, the relationship isn't worth it?" Ryan asked, "That hardly seems fair to Audrey or Abby. I don't need to have known Abby for years to know that I love her."

"I'm not saying you shouldn't search for her," Tony said, "I am just worried about how far you are going to take this. Your search for her has involved military and men in suits, or in other words, dangerous people."

"Now that sounds a lot like you don't want me to search for her," Ryan said, "If you keep talking such nonsense, I am going to have to quit listening to you entirely. I am not going to stop my search and I know how to be careful."

Ryan got up from the stool and went back to his office. He left Tony sitting there with the rest of the pizza. Tony did not say anything to stop him. Since he had some of the pizza, Ryan did not stop working until he was too tired to concentrate and had to get some sleep.

Ryan woke to a headache and the phone ringing. He groaned as he turned on to his side. The phone was a short distance away, but it stopped ringing so Ryan dropped his arm. He lay there trying to remember if he had done anything to deserve the headache. He didn't remember drinking or getting drunk. There might be some jetlag from the trip to talk to Selena's brother.

There was a knock on the door. Ryan looked up to see Tony standing there. He didn't have the phone in hand.

"Who was it?" Ryan asked.

"I don't know," Tony answered, "He didn't identify himself. All he said was she is gone."

"What did his voice sound like?" Ryan asked.

"Quiet, normal," Tony shrugged.

"What was the number?" Ryan asked.

"It was blocked," Tony answered.

"Okay," Ryan said as he closed his eyes against the pounding on his temples.

"Are you going back to sleep?" Tony asked, "Because then I should tell you that I am going out and don't know when I will be back."

"That is fine," Ryan said, "Less noise to bother my headache."

"I'll leave you alone then," Tony said.

Tony left the doorway. Several minutes later, Ryan heard the apartment door open and close. Ryan rolled over to get more comfortable and then tried to go back to sleep. Despite the pain, it didn't take long before he drifted off.

Something disturbed Ryan's sleep and caused him to turn back towards the door of his room. He attempted to try and figure out what woke him. His head was still pounding making it harder. Ryan remembered that Tony had left earlier. Whatever woke him did not repeat, so Ryan crawled out of bed.

Ryan suddenly felt light-headed and almost passed out. He sat back down on the bed. Sitting there, he felt nausea and the vomit rising in his throat. Ryan swallowed it. Despite that, it rose again. Ryan stood up and tried to get across his room to the door. He only got half-way before collapsing to the floor.

Managing to keep the bile down, Ryan crawled the rest of the way across the floor. He did not try to get up and instead crawled the rest of the way to the toilet. Only once his head was over the bowl did he open his mouth and let his system do what it wanted.

When Ryan felt his system was finished, he lay down on the bathroom floor. The cold of the tile was nice on his skin. His headache was not as bad now. In fact, he was feeling better. But Ryan did not move in case it was all an illusion and started to feel worse again.

All this meant was the headache had nothing to do with jetlag. Nausea and emptying of the stomach suggested food poisoning. He wondered if Tony was suffering from any symptoms. He had seemed to be healthy when he had said he was going out. It did not make sense to be food poisoning as it usually did not include light-headedness and headache.

Maybe it was best for him to stay on the bathroom floor. The tile had cooled him down, so he was nice and cold while being too cold. Ryan reached up and pulled the bath mat on top of him. Then he closed his eyes and relaxed.

"Ryan?" Tony's voice came from above. Ryan opened his eyes and looked up at his friend's face.

"Yeah?" Ryan asked.

"What are you doing on the bathroom floor?" Tony asked.

"I wasn't feeling well," Ryan sat up and pushed the bath mat off him, "And I was feeling better after coming in here so I stayed."

"Are you feeling better now?" Tony asked.

"The headache hasn't completely disappeared but other than that I am," Ryan answered. He carefully got to his feet. There was no light-headedness or nausea, so he stayed upright. The only, aside from the headache, he was feeling thirsty.

"What time is it?" Ryan asked as he made his way to the kitchen. Tony followed him.

"Suppertime," Tony answered, "I was trying to figure out what to eat and thought you might have an idea so I went looking for you."

"I need a few minutes to figure out if I am even

hungry," Ryan said. He poured some water into a glass before sitting down on a stool. Ryan sipped the water.

"You should eat something if you can keep it down," Tony said, "How about I warm up a can of chicken soup?"

"Sure," Ryan said. He took another sip of water. Tony got busy putting the soup on. Once the soup was on the stove, Tony sat down on the other stool.

"Did Hagan stop by with more information?" Tony asked.

"If he did, I slept through it," Ryan answered.

"He has been stopping by so regularly I thought he would do so today as well," Tony said.

"Maybe he didn't have any new information to share," Ryan said, "Where did you spend the day?"

"Work," Tony answered, "I have to do that occasionally if I expect to be paid."

"They still let you in?" Ryan asked.

"My boss likes me too much to let my supervisor lock me out," Tony responded, "Which is good because I have bills to pay."

The phone rang. Ryan got up to get it.

"Hello?"

"Hey, Ryan," Jey's voice came through, "I know you've been busy, but Savanna suggested inviting you to our gig tonight. She thought you shouldn't be left alone too much."

"I spent the day sick," Ryan said, "I'm not sure it is a good idea to go out as much as I feel better now."

"Sometimes an exchange of air helps," Jey said, "Come out. You don't need to drink, just come and enjoy the music."

Ryan thought about it for a moment. He was feeling

better and getting out would likely be a good thing.

"Sure," Ryan said, "Where is the gig?"

"The usual place," Jey answered.

"Not yet moved on to bigger and better?" Ryan asked.

"We are still trying out some new stuff and we want to make sure it is okay with our fans before taking the songs too far," Jey said.

"So, there'll be new songs this evening?" Ryan asked.

"Probably a couple you haven't heard before," Jey answered.

"Shall be a good show then," Ryan said, "See you there."

"You'll be expected," Jey said before hanging up.

Ryan got up and the handset away before sitting back down. Tony got up to stir and check the soup. Finding it not ready to eat yet, he sat back down.

"Jey inviting you out?" Tony asked.

"Yeah," Ryan answered, "Want to come? It will get you out of the apartment for an evening."

"Why not," Tony said, "Do we have time to eat?"

"We have a while," Ryan answered, "I don't plan to drink much, if anything, as I don't want to cause myself to be sick again."

"I probably shouldn't have much myself," Tony said, "It would probably be rude not to have one at least."

"I'm not going to tell you what to drink and what not to drink," Ryan said, "I'm just saying I won't be. Others there are a different matter, if you dislike drinking alone."

"We'll see," Tony said. He got up and checked on

the soup again. This time he decided it was warm enough and dished it up.

After they were finished eating, Ryan cleaned up from the meal. Tony went to the living room. As Ryan was finishing up in the kitchen, he could hear Tony talking quietly. He couldn't hear specific words and he didn't try. Ryan went to his room long enough to gather his keys and wallet. After a stop in the bathroom, Ryan got his shoes and coat on. Once Tony was ready, the two of them left the apartment.

When they arrived at the club, Ryan paid the cover charge for Tony and were let inside. Savanna was already seated at a booth with a good view of the stage.

"Hey," Ryan said as he and Tony sat down, "You remember my friend Tony."

"I do," Savanna nodded to him.

"Nice to see you again," Tony said, "How are you doing?"

"Back in high school, I found myself in paranoid state at far too regular intervals," Savanna said, "But I had mostly recovered from that since I was eighteen. That was until the last couple of days."

"I know the search for Abby has caused plenty of reasons for paranoia," Ryan said, "But what else is causing them?"

"The last couple days I feel like I am being followed," Savanna answered, "It is starting to affect my mental health."

"Do you know whether it is just a feeling or whether you are actually being followed?" Ryan asked.

"Occasionally, when I look back I think I can see someone move out of my sight," Savanna answered, "But I'm never completely sure that I am actually seeing it because in the past I have seen things out of the corner of my eyes that wasn't there. It hasn't been as much of a problem lately, but it is still in my mind."

"Has Jey noticed the feeling or a person?" Ryan asked.

"He keeps trying to reassure me, but I've noticed him glancing around as if he is feeling it as well," Savanna answered, "Adam started to make a comment that sounded like he had noticed someone following us, but Jay gave him a look that shut him up. I understand Jey trying to protect me, however, it is just causing me a level of anxiety I haven't felt since high school and hoped to never feel again." Her hands were shaking and she tried to stop it by setting them flat on the table.

Ryan started looking for a waitress when one arrived at the table. Savanna and Tony ordered alcoholic drinks while Ryan ordered a drink that was not. The waitress left them to get their drinks.

"Are you being followed?" Savanna asked.

"I haven't noticed anyone," Ryan answered, "But there was a man with a suit watching my apartment. I haven't seen him lately. The last time I came to a performance, we were followed back to my place."

"True," Savanna said, "I think it was after that evening that I started to feel it. Now I feel like it all the time. I would be doing better if Jey would admit to feeling it too because then I would feel less like I am going crazy."

"I doubt it is just you feeling it," Ryan said, "But it doesn't make much sense for Jey not to talk to you on the matter. He is usually better at communicating than that."

"I've been trying not to, but the thought that he

knows more about the situation and just doesn't want to admit it," Savanna said, "He has never done that in the past, nor is it like him to do such a thing. Such thoughts spin around my head when my paranoia shows up. His attempts to calm those thoughts are making things worse."

"Maybe we can talk to him about it," Ryan said.

"You can try," Savanna said.

Anymore conversation was interrupted by the opening act started up. Ryan hadn't heard the group before and with the volume they were playing at he wasn't sure he was going to hear again. He noticed Savanna wince at the noise and Tony looked ready to plug his ears.

Tony shouted something to Ryan, but Ryan couldn't hear what it was. He leaned closer to Tony and cupped his hand to his ear. Tony leaned close before trying again.

"I hope it is a short opener."

"Agreed," Ryan shouted back with a nod.

With nothing else to do, they watched the band while Savanna and Tony had several more drinks. Ryan thought about switching to something with alcohol in it, but decided to give his system a break it seemed to need.

Ryan was started to ache from the bass pounding through his chest when Oscar sat down on the other side of the booth. Oscar nodded to Ryan and Ryan nodded back. There was no point in trying to talk anyway.

This was the last song for the opener and the club manager was hurrying them off the stage on his way to the microphone to announce Smash. Once the sound stopped, Ryan felt exhausted from the pounding. Tony slumped a little as if the music was what was holding him up. Savanna finished her drink and signalled the waitress for another.

"What was that?" Ryan asked as the band members of Smash set up as quickly as they could.

"Noise pollution," Oscar answered.

"Is that the name of the band or the description of the music?" Tony asked.

"I don't know the name of the band," Oscar answered.

"Okay," Tony nodded.

Smash started playing and everyone relaxed while they enjoyed the music. The waitress brought the next round of drinks; two alcoholic and two non-alcoholic. Oscar raised his eyebrows at Ryan.

"I was feeling sick earlier," Ryan said.

Oscar nodded.

Now that his body was not being assaulted, Ryan could feel someone watching them. Without moving his head and trying to still appear relaxed, Ryan looked around the club. Most of the people were paying attention to the band and the music. There were plenty who were visiting with each other. Nothing about their table for it to attract attention, so no one's eyes stayed on them. But there was lots of the club Ryan could not see without turning his head and he did not want to do anything that would give away that he was looking.

Ryan realized that Oscar was aware they were being watched as well. However, Oscar was doing nothing to try and find the person in the club. Since Oscar was relaxed and not bothered by whoever was watching them, Ryan relaxed slightly and focused on the performance.

At the break, Oscar got up and went backstage. The waitress arrived with another round of drinks. The feeling started to bother Ryan again.

"You two feel it, right?" Savanna asked.

"Yes," Tony answered. Ryan nodded.

"So, I'm not crazy," Savanna slumped down a little bit, "I was starting to wonder."

"I don't know why Jey or anyone else is not willing to admit it, but you aren't crazy in feeling like you are being watched," Ryan said, "But I haven't been able to see the person."

"You can find anyone in this crowd?" Savanna asked.

"It helps when everyone is focused on the band," Ryan answered, "Because then there are a limited number of people not paying attention to the stage."

"I guess that makes sense," Savanna said. She took another sip of her drink as she seemed to think it over.

"I will have to wait until the band starts again to see if I can identify who is watching," Ryan said.

"Oscar was facing the other direction," Tony said, "Wouldn't he have noticed someone?"

"He isn't likely to tell us anything," Savanna said, "Or at least these days it seems the whole band isn't willing to talk to me about the matter."

Ryan almost said something but decided it was better not to. He thought about having a drink, but did not. His attention wandered back to the others in the club and only half-an-ear to Tony and Savanna. He was still not able to see anyone who might be watching the table. Finally, an idea came to him.

"I'm going to the bathroom," Ryan told Tony. Tony

nodded but was not really paying attention. Ryan got up and headed to the area where the restrooms were. He kept an eye on the patrons. Most were busy and the few who were not busy looking for something else. None of them were what Ryan was watching for. Then Ryan saw the man. The man was paying attention to the table where Tony and Savanna were seated. He had a drink in his hand, but appeared not to notice it. The man appeared to be in his late teens or early twenties. He had light brown hair that fell over his forehead. His face had an intensity as he watched the table. There were too many people between Ryan and the man, so Ryan decided knowing what the man looked like was enough.

Ryan went to the bathroom and then headed back to the table. By the time he got back, Oscar was there. The server brought another round of drinks. Once she was gone, the break was over and the band came back on. Ryan relaxed and enjoyed the music. Oscar was relaxed as well, but not as much as Ryan.

By the time the music was done, Tony and Savanna were well drunk and Ryan was missing being the same. Ryan now understood how Oscar felt when he had to put up with everyone else at the end of the evening. Jey and the rest of the band joined them at the table. A few audience members came up to the table to say how much they liked the band and ask for autographs. Oscar let them come as there were only a few. Then they were left to drink.

"How are things going?" Jey asked.

"Not as well as I would like," Ryan answered.

"No progress on finding Abby?" Jey asked.

"No progress," Ryan answered.

"I really hoped that with Hagan's help you would

have something," Jey said.

"He has been quite helpful," Ryan said, "But this search is harder than I thought it would be."

"Hopefully, things get better soon," Jey said.

"Everything okay with you?" Ryan asked.

"Yeah," Jey answered.

"Then what is up with you making Savanna feel like she is going crazy?" Ryan asked.

"I don't mean to," Jey answered.

"There is someone who has been watching the table all evening," Ryan said, "Savanna said she has felt it a lot recently, but you have denied her feelings in this matter."

"Yeah, there has been someone following the band around," Jey said, "But I have been trying to prevent Savanna from worrying over the matter."

"Might be best to just sit down and have a talk with her," Ryan said, "Because you know what happens to relationships when there is a lack of communication."

"Yeah," Jey said with a nod.

"This evening she said that she felt like she was going crazy because you were denying what she was feeling," Ryan said.

"That is not good," Jey said as he glanced over to Savanna, who was still talking to Tony. They had found a topic they both knew about and were interested in.

"Not drinking?" the keyboardist asked Ryan.

"I wasn't feeling well earlier," Ryan answered, "So, I thought it best if I skip the booze tonight."

"You don't know that alcohol makes people feel better?" the keyboardist asked.

"Have you tried it?" Ryan asked.

"No," the keyboardist answered, "But my grandpa

always swore by it. He liked his whiskey and his hot toddies and the occasional barley sandwich for lunch."

"Was he an alcoholic?" Ryan asked.

"No, he just liked to drink," the keyboardist answered, "He was most likely to drink on Fridays, but he abstained the rest of the week. In fact, he never drank on Saturdays as so not have any obstacles to going to church on Sunday. I can order you something that will make you feel better."

"Fine," Ryan said.

The keyboardist called the server over and he gave her the drink order. She nodded and then went off to get it. It was not long before she was back with it. Ryan looked it over, but it just appeared to golden liquid in a clear glass. It did not smell strongly of anything. Ryan took a sip. It was not as strong as he feared, but it definitely made him feel better.

"Well?" the keyboardist asked.

"Tastes good," Ryan answered.

"The second mouthful is stronger," the keyboardist said as Ryan raised the glass. He took another sip and found the warning to be correct.

"Yeah," Ryan breathed out. It went down smooth and then the effects spread throughout his body. The drink was strong but it left him feeling good. He did not rush to finish it though. The rest of the band and Tony drank together.

By the time Ryan was finished his drink, the club had stopped serving drinks. They were not rushing people out yet, but encouraging people to leave and come back tomorrow night. Once everyone else was finished their drinks, they got ready to go.

"We should call a cab," the keyboardist said as they

headed towards the door.

"Okay, call," Jey said. The keyboardist started searching his pockets for his phone. He could not find it.

"I guess not," the keyboardist said.

They stepped out onto the sidewalk and the evening air felt good. Ryan used his shoulder to keep Tony from collapsing to the sidewalk. Tony was doing well to keep himself up but he could not go in a straight line. Jey was supporting Savanna. The whole group headed down the sidewalk without really agreeing on a destination.

"We are being followed again," the keyboardist said. Ryan had not noticed the feeling after the drink, but now that it was mentioned he felt it again.

"Been there all evening," Tony said, "But couldn't see who."

"Maybe we should call Oscar," Chase said.

"He already went home," the keyboardist said, "And he doesn't like to drive us when we have been drinking."

"He knows we were watched all night and didn't do anything," Savanna said, "I doubt he wants to be disturbed over it."

Maybe it was the drink, or the couple weeks, but Ryan felt really tired of being followed. He got Chase to support Tony and then stepped into a dark area near the storefronts. The rest of the group kept going as most of them did not even notice he was gone. They were just about to the end of the block before the person following them came passed Ryan. It was the man Ryan had noticed in the club.

Ryan stepped forward and grabbed the man by the

arm. He pushed the man against the building and put his forearm against the man's throat. The man struggled against Ryan but was not strong enough to break free. The group had heard the scuffle and came back.

"Who are you?" Ryan demanded.

"Austin Lewis," the man choked out.

"Why are you following us?" Ryan demanded.

"I needed to talk to the band," Austin answered.

"What?" Jey asked, "Why?"

"You are my sister's favourite band," Austin answered, "And I wanted to ask if you would play for her, but when I tried calling your manager, he told me no and to stay away from you."

Ryan released Austin from the chokehold but did not step back. Austin massaged his neck for a moment and did not try to move.

"You talked to Randall?" Jey asked.

"Yes," Austin answered, "And I have been trying to work up my nerve to try and talk to you. I didn't dare try while the bodyguard was around."

"I told you Randall didn't have our best interests in mind," Chase said.

"Yeah, you did," Jey said, "But we already signed the contract. Why doesn't your sister just come to the show?"

"She is in the hospital," Austin answered, "She has been diagnosed with terminal cancer and she has been too sick to be moved."

Jey was sober enough to understand the whole situation. Ryan glanced at Jey and saw the pain flicker over his face. Jey's mother had died from cancer and he had spent the last several months by her bedside. He would have done anything and everything to relieve his mother's suffering, even for a minute.

"It is a little late for us to play for her now," Jey said, "But there should be plenty tomorrow afternoon. Give me your number and we can arrange it." Jey took out his cell. Austin gave his number and Jey put it into his contacts.

"I am sorry about Randall," Jey said, "He is a big city manager and middle management intelligence."

"Katie will be so happy," Austin said. He looked relieved as to how this whole situation was going.

"It is always good to meet our fans," Chase said.

"Thank you," Austin said, "I appreciate it so much."

"Then I will call you," Jey said, "And we will see you tomorrow."

"See you tomorrow," Austin said. Then he went off.

"You think Oscar knew about Austin?" Chase asked.

"We are about to find out," Jey answered as he pushed a button and put his phone to his ear. The group waited.

"It is Jey. You wouldn't happen to know about a young man with the name of Austin Lewis?" Jey was quiet as he listened to Oscar's response. "We just confronted him about following us." Jey stayed quiet for a minute. "He was stalking us, but only because Randall denied him access. Come pick us up and we'll explain everything." Jey listened to the response and then ended the call.

"We don't have to walk home?" the keyboardist asked.

"He is coming to pick us up," Jey answered.

"Great," the keyboardist said.

"Why did you do that?" Jey asked Ryan.

"I'm getting tired of being followed around by

strange people," Ryan answered, "Though I think this time ended a lot happier than any other time will."

"This did end well," Jey said.

"We need to have a long talk with Randall," Chase said.

"Yeah, we do," Jey said, "You would think that he would want us to talk with fans rather than avoiding them."

"Apparently, he is worried about your fans stalking you and having bad intentions," Ryan said.

"We aren't," Jey said, "Now we have to be worried about Randall separating us from fans who need us."

"At least no one is following us," Savanna said.

"True," Jey said, "That part is dealt with."

"And a ride home," Savanna said.

"Yeah," Jey said, "If he can find us. I forgot to tell him where we are."

The group laughed. They started back in the direction of the club.

They were still a short distance when Oscar pulled to the curb in his van. The group climbed in. Jey explained what all had happened as Oscar drove. Ryan did not pay much attention. He felt like he could relax for a moment. Tony actually had to poke him when they reached his apartment building because Ryan was not paying attention. He and Tony got out of the van, waved goodbye, and then headed up to the apartment. After getting into the apartment, Ryan locked the door before heading straight to bed. He closed his eyes and was out shortly.

CHAPTER FIVE

The phone rang. Ryan started to raise his head, but was quick to put it back down as the sick feeling washed over him. He had no trouble remembering the night before and Ryan was sure he had been tired but not drunk enough to be hungover now. The phone stopped and Ryan closed his eyes. He drifted back to sleep because it was easiest.

"Ryan," Tony's voice interrupted the drift. Ryan tried to fight his way to wakefulness, but he was wrapped in cotton.

"Ryan!" Tony grabbed Ryan's shoulder and shook it hard.

"What?" Ryan could hear the muffled sound in his own voice.

"You need to get up," Tony said.

"Why?" Ryan asked.

"Come on," Tony said, "Come out to the living room."

"Why?" Ryan asked.

"Come on," Tony answered pulling on Ryan's arm. Ryan wanted to be left alone to go back to sleep, but some part of his brain suggested he would not be left alone unless he did something about Tony. Despite the cotton feeling, Ryan sat up and opened his eyes. Slowly he got to his feet and followed Tony out to the living room. Ryan sat down in the chair and immediately slumped down. His eyes drifted closed. This time Tony left him alone to sleep.

There was a knock at the door and someone nearby moved. The cotton feeling was gone as Ryan opened his eyes and lifted his head. There was less tiredness and the sick feeling was gone. Tony came back into the living room. He was followed by Hagan, who sat down in the other chair. Ryan looked at Hagan and saw that he appeared pale.

"You didn't call yesterday," Ryan said.

"No, I didn't," Hagan said, "I barely made it out of bed and that was long enough to empty my stomach into a bucket."

"I was sick yesterday, too," Ryan said.

"I figured as much," Hagan said, "That is why I phoned this morning. I might not have done that if my friend had not stopped by."

"What?" Ryan asked. Something Hagan was saying was triggering alarms in Ryan's head, but it was foggy enough he could not figure out why.

"I am suffering from CO2 poisoning," Hagan said, "And it seems like you might be too."

"How?" Ryan asked, "Tony isn't sick."

"Do you have an air vent in your bedroom?" Hagan

asked.

"Yes," Ryan answered.

"That is likely the how," Hagan said, "I found the canister in my air vent. It looked like something that might belong to the military."

"You think the people who took Abby are trying to kill us?" Ryan asked.

"Maybe," Hagan answered, "Or distracted enough to drop the search."

"We need to deal with the one in my room," Ryan said.

"We do," Hagan said, "I know how to do it." He got up and headed down the hallway. Ryan wanted to follow him, but he was not sure whether his legs could work. There was the sound of metal on metal and then it was repeated. Another moment went by before Hagan came out carrying a canister. He set it down on the coffee table before sitting down again.

"That is scary," Tony said looking at it, "You two could have died."

"That is why I was okay yesterday evening," Ryan said, "Because I spent the afternoon in the bathroom and away from the canister."

"You might have saved your own life by doing that," Tony said.

"Are you going to be okay?" Ryan asked Hagan.

"I will recover," Hagan answered, "My friend found the canister and he is airing my place out. I left him beside an open window and he will let me know when the place is safe for me to return. Until then, I have another place I can stay."

"Okay," Ryan said with a nod.

"I am sorry that I have not been able to work on the

case," Hagan said.

"Based on current issues, I understand why," Ryan said.

"I will go back to looking into things now that I am not sick," Hagan said.

"Are you sure you want to?" Tony asked.

"Most definitely," Hagan answered, "Attempting to hurt me, just makes me want to finish the job."

Tony turned to Ryan and opened his mouth to say something. Ryan shook his head.

"No, I'm not going to demand a stop to this search," Ryan said, "We have come too far to turn back now."

"They managed to get into your apartment without you or anyone else knowing about it," Tony said, "And if they had put more canisters here, they might have actually killed you. Likely me as well."

"They got into the apartment to steal Abby right out of my bed without me knowing about it," Ryan said, "I am not surprised they managed to put the canister in here. Also, if they did want to kill me, I would likely be dead already."

"They are warning you away," Tony said, "Shouldn't you listen?"

"That just means we have their attention," Hagan said, "Now we have to convince them we mean business and we aren't going to go away. Some of those agencies will provide information to get rid of people asking questions. Some will and some are good at covering up murder."

"I'm sorry, but CO_2 poisoning sounds more like the type good at covering up murder than providing information," Tony said.

"I think you are taking this incident out of context,"

Ryan said.

"Someone poisoned you and I am taking it out of context?" Tony asked.

"Yes," Ryan answered, "You see it as attempted murder and they mean it as a distraction."

"If you had gotten any worse, you would have been dead," Tony said.

"It is easy to take it out of context," Ryan said, "And I'm not saying there isn't any danger. But they are not actively trying to kill me or Hagan. If they were, we would already be dead."

"And the word poisoning doesn't suggest to you that continuing this search is a bad thing?" Tony asked.

"He isn't getting it," Hagan said before Ryan could say anything else. Ryan nodded as he realized Hagan was right.

"I'm not stopping the search," Ryan said, "Their threat doesn't scare me. If it worries you then you will need to find somewhere else to live. I don't mind having someone here to keep an eye on the place and I don't want to send you away, so the decision is up to you."

Tony stared at Ryan for a long moment as he thought the matter over. There was fear in his eyes and Ryan knew the CO_2 poisoning was the point on which Tony would decide. Ryan did not blame him as this made things real and Tony had already been worried about the matter.

"I will stay around," Tony said finally, "But I am still nervous over this matter."

"Nervousness is understandable," Ryan said, "I am glad you decided to stay."

"I have a session with my therapist," Tony said. He

stood up and left the living room. Ryan and Hagan heard him leave the apartment.

"Are you sure you want him around?" Hagan asked, "His nervousness could turn out to be a bit of a problem."

"It will be okay," Ryan said, "And it will be a good thing to have someone else in the apartment."

"It was useful earlier," Hagan said, "I need to leave too. Hopefully, I will have the information for you tomorrow."

"I hope so, too," Ryan said.

They both got up and Ryan showed Hagan out. He locked the door. Ryan found something to eat and some coffee then went to his office to get some work done.

It was late afternoon when the phone rang and interrupted Ryan's work. Since he had not heard Tony return, Ryan assumed he was not home. Ryan picked up the phone.

"Hello?"

"You remember Katie Unger?" Jey asked.

"Sure," Ryan answered, "She wore the purple Mohawk and stood by the stage so she could dance without anyone complaining. She didn't drink much, but she had fun."

"She is Austin's sister," Jey said.

"That sucks," Ryan said.

"Yeah," Jey said.

"But that does explain why she quit coming to shows," Ryan said.

"It does," Jey said, "She had managed to keep the Mohawk, but most of the purple was gone. Apparently, no one noticed any symptoms of cancer until one day she collapsed. Now the doctor says she is terminal. She has been keeping her spirits up as best she can, but living in the hospital doesn't help much."

"How did she enjoy you playing?" Ryan asked.

"She was so excited," Jey answered, "Her parents were quite as much, but seeing her happy made them let us stay. We were able to play for a couple hours in between talking to her. She was happy about what we are doing as she feels that the world needs to hear our music. It was good to hear that and I think we needed to hear it."

"How did the talk with your new manager go?" Ryan asked.

"I think he understands why he shouldn't cut us off from our fans," Jey answered, "And he also understands that if we find out that he has done it again, he will not be our manager anymore."

"I hope he understands that the band isn't desperate enough to accept just any behaviour," Ryan said.

"I thought he did when we signed the contract," Jey said, "But we repeated it again today when we talked to him. So, hopefully, now, he will understand. The whole band stood there in his office and offered to rip up the contract and walk out if he ever did that again. He tried to argue, but we stood our ground on the matter. Having just come from the hospital and visiting Katie there was no way we were going to bend."

"You had a good afternoon?" Ryan asked.

"The whole band did," Jey answered, "It was sad to leave Katie because we are not sure we will ever see her again. Her doctor is not sure how long she has. She says she wants to come to hear us play if she ever gets out of the hospital. We would welcome that, but it is unlikely she will ever get out. We are playing tonight, are you coming?"

"I'll think about it," Ryan said, "I have to get some work done and I'm not sure when I will be able to take a break."

"Understandable," Jey said, "You have been working on other things and distracted by more important matters. You were sick yesterday, are you still suffering from those effects?"

"I haven't fully recovered," Ryan said, "But I know the cause now and it will go away."

"That sounds concerning," Jey said, "Maybe you do need some time away."

"Maybe," Ryan said, "But I do need to get some work done."

"Well, then I will let you go and you can get enough work done so that you can come this evening," Jey said, "I expect to see you there."

"Okay," Ryan said. Jey hung up. Ryan got up and went out to the kitchen. Tony was not there. Ryan poured himself another cup of coffee, grabbed a snack, and went back to his desk.

Ryan's concentration was interrupted again, but this time by the noise of someone coming into the apartment. Noting that it was suppertime, Ryan took his coffee cup to the kitchen. Tony was sitting at the counter and eating pizza out of the box.

"How was your day?" Tony asked as Ryan put his coffee cup on the counter by the sink.

"I spent it working," Ryan answered, "I need to keep money coming in to make sure I can keep paying for things. How was your therapy session?"

"I don't know anymore," Tony said, "I thought there was progress and now I really don't know. Then I went to work for a few hours."

"How did that go?" Ryan asked.

"The usual," Tony said with a shrug, "Are you going out tonight?"

"Jey is expecting me at the show tonight," Ryan answered, "I was trying to get enough work done to take the evening off."

"Did you manage it?" Tony asked.

"Close enough at this point," Ryan answered.

"Have some pizza and we can go together," Tony said.

"Are you sure about it?" Ryan asked, "I wouldn't want to interrupt anything you need to do tomorrow."

"I think it was helpful to get out last night," Tony said, "My therapist keeps saying I should get out and do things without Audrey. Not sure Smash is my type of music, but it was nice to get out."

"Okay," Ryan said as he sat down at the counter. He took a piece of pizza and started eating.

"So, Jey called?" Tony asked.

"They played for Austin's sister this afternoon," Ryan answered, "They also threatened their manager. Everything worked out, except for the part where a fan of theirs is dying from cancer."

"Good," Tony said, "I am surprised at you confronting the man following them."

"I'm getting really tired of being followed by strange people," Ryan said, "I tried to confront the guy who was watching my apartment from across the road, but he disappeared before I could reach him. I haven't noticed if he has been back."

"I haven't noticed anyone out there," Tony said, "But I haven't been paying attention. Has he been following you other places?"

"Not that I have noticed," Ryan answered, "At least in confronting the man last night, there was a happy ending."

"You don't think there will be a happy ending when or if you confront the man who was watching from across the street?" Tony asked.

"Maybe it is just the pessimist in me," Ryan answered, "But no, I don't there will be a happy ending. It might have something to do with my girlfriend having been kidnapped and there have been threats against my life since I started searching for her. I would like to talk to the man because if he knows something I want to know it and if he can direct me to where she is, it would be even better."

"I guess that makes sense," Tony said, "But it does sound dangerous."

"Yeah, but I would do it for answers," Ryan said.

Tony nodded and did not add anything else. They finished the pizza. Then they got ready to go.

Tony and Ryan did not have any trouble finding the table where Savanna was sitting there drinking. They both ordered alcohol when the server stopped at the table. Savanna nodded at them.

"How are you doing tonight?" Ryan asked.

"Better," Savanna answered, "Jey and I managed to talk over what was going on. He will not make any attempts to prevent me from worrying anymore."

"That is good," Ryan said.

"Sometimes I think he needs something big to

happen before he remembers to communicate," Savanna said, "But I love him anyway."

"As long as you no longer feel like you are going crazy," Ryan said.

"Not in that way anymore," Savanna said, "Just the normal stuff. How is the search for Abby?"

"Not getting very far right now," Ryan answered, "I went and talked to her brother, but he hasn't heard from her since high school when they were put into different foster homes."

"They should have been put into the same foster home as siblings," Savanna said, "But it doesn't happen. I'm not surprised Abby was a foster child. Occasionally she showed signs of being too independent and questioning authority suggestive of someone who had been betrayed by adults when she was young. What was he like?"

'He was concerned about her," Ryan said, "And he hopes that she would be interested in visiting him if I find her."

"Depends a lot on how badly she wants to forget the past," Savanna said, "If you are supportive of the visit, she might be okay with it."

"We will see how she is when I find her," Ryan said.

"True," Savanna said, "She has been gone for a week or so and anything could have happened to her."

"I'm hoping not too much has happened to her yet," Ryan said, "But I have been focused on finding her more than what she is going through."

"That is understandable," Savanna said, "I really hope you find her soon."

"So do I," Ryan said.

Oscar came out from backstage and sat down. He

nodded hello to Ryan and Tony. Ryan nodded back. Smash came out on stage and started playing.

"No opener?" Ryan asked.

"The club couldn't find one," Savanna answered, "The manager asked if it was okay and the band was okay with it."

Ryan nodded before relaxing to enjoy the show.

It has been a great show and a great evening. The biggest problem Ryan had was missing having Abby there to enjoy it with him. Being there with Tony just was not the same. The only one who was not buzzed was Oscar, who had not been drinking. Jey and Chase came out after the show and joined them. Oscar went backstage to help pack up the band's stuff.

"How you doing?" Jey asked Ryan.

"Right now, well," Ryan answered, "Enough booze will do that, especially when it doesn't feel like someone is watching."

"That does help," Jey said.

"I do miss my girlfriend," Ryan said.

"Expected," Jey said, "Did Hagan contact you today?"

"Yes," Ryan answered, "He didn't contact me yesterday because he was sick, but he claims he will make up for it."

"He will," Jey said, "He doesn't like things that put him behind schedule."

"He said as much," Ryan said.

Jey nodded but he was distracted by his drink arriving. Chase asked Ryan a question about something else entirely and that was the end of the conversation about Hagan.

Once closing time was announced, Oscar gave everyone a ride home. He did not let anyone distract him from getting them home without stopping anywhere unnecessarily. Ryan and Tony used each other as support to get up to Ryan's apartment. Ryan locked the door before leaving, Tony headed to the living room and went off to his bedroom. He stopped in the doorway long enough to remove his shoes and jacket before crawling into bed.

Ryan thought he would fall asleep right away, but instead found himself staring at the other side of the bed. It was empty. Ryan reached over and felt the bedding. It was indeed empty. Abby was not there. He felt in his chest that she should be there. She would be a drunk as he was and she would be laughing while discussing the highlights of the show. The bed beside him should be filled with excitement, energy, and beauty; the eyes glittering with life and hair falling over her naked body. He could reach out and take some hair to play with. She would giggle when he tickled her with it. Why was she gone? Where had she gone? Ryan's eyes drifted closed.

Ryan slowly opened his eyes to see the other side of the bed was empty. It seemed wrong. The window showed that day had arrived, but the cloudiness suggested the weather was not the best. Abby would usually snuggle up to him and suggest they go back to sleep. Ryan wanted to, but Abby was not in bed to snuggle with.

Slowly Ryan sat up. His bladder and his head were not comfortable, so he might as well deal with them. After a stop in the bathroom, Ryan went out to the kitchen for water and painkillers. He could not hear Tony moving, so he went to his office and got to work.

When he heard Tony moving around, Ryan went back out to the kitchen for another glass of water. Tony did not look ready to deal with the world, so Ryan went back to his office to get more work done. Despite the hangover and his chest hurting, Ryan was actually getting plenty of work done. It was almost enough to make up for the day he was sick.

At lunch, Ryan went out to the kitchen. He found Tony sitting at the counter with his head in his hands.

"I thought you would be gone to your therapy session or work," Ryan said.

"I called in sick," Tony replied.

"Can you afford to do that?" Ryan asked.

"I don't know," Tony asked, "But I know that my body can and can't do."

"Tried painkillers?" Ryan asked.

"Yeah, but they didn't help much," Tony answered, "You aren't planning to make a lot of noise today, are you?"

"I expect Hagan to drop in with information," Ryan said, "Other than that, I was planning to work."

"Then I am going to attempt sleep again," Tony said as he got up. Before he could move any farther, there was a knock on the door.

"That is probably Hagan," Ryan said before heading for the door. Tony headed for the living room. Ryan checked the peephole and saw that is was Hagan, so he unlocked and opened the door.

"Come in," Ryan said as he stepped out of the way. Hagan entered. Ryan closed the door before leading into the kitchen. They sat down on stools at the counter.

"So, the school," Hagan said as he took some papers out of his bag, "The Platt Truman school for Exceptional Students. It seems to exist on paper and other students have been accepted into it, but where the students go is unknown. All students who are accepted lack family situations where people ask questions. Also, all students lack funding and the letters received for the students tells of funding provided for them."

"So, it was not sure Abby who was accepted into this school?" Ryan asked.

"No, there were several I have managed to track down," Hagan answered, "All of them were similar. In fact, at least one was also a foster child of the Warners. His name was Jeremiah Golden. His parents had died a few months before he was put with the Warners."

"Died of what?" Ryan asked.

"A climbing accident," Hagan answered, "The whole family went on vacation and he was the only one to return. There wasn't any family who could take him in and he was placed in foster care. Then a letter arrived about him from the school. He was picked up and never heard from again."

"Nothing?" Ryan asked.

"Nothing," Hagan confirmed, "Like Abby, he may have changed his identity and that would make it almost impossible to find him. But I don't think it was chance that two foster children from the same place disappeared as after both Jeremiah and Abby disappeared, the Warners received money from an anonymous source."

"So, they were paid to give these kids up to this fake school," Ryan said.

"Yes," Hagan said, "I researched who Platt Truman

was and he was an actual person. He was a government employee but there is no information about what part of the government he worked for or what his job was."

"That could mean that the government is behind all these disappearances," Ryan said.

"It seems like it," Hagan said, "But because I can't find out where he worked, I'm having trouble getting any information on him. Unfortunately, when requesting information through the government it is not enough to just have a name. Since the school doesn't really exist, they are unwilling to provide information on that."

"Is it still running?" Ryan asked, "As in, are students still being sent there?"

"Not that I can find," Hagan answered, "They stopped accepting children into the school about five years after Abby was taken. Shortly after the Warners were caught doing things of questionable nature to add funds to their family, Liza especially. Their accreditation as foster parents were pulled and no children were left in their care. Lindsay Wilson, and her husband Frank, have been foster parents for about five years and there have been no complaints against them as of yet."

"But they liked haven't changed anything other than their names," Ryan said.

"There is a large problem with the system," Hagan said, "A social worker has to determine that there are serious issues in the foster home before they will do something and without any complaints they won't do anything."

"Which is only going to happen if there is evidence," Ryan said, "Unless they are a problem with finding

Abby, I don't care what happens to them."

"Do you want to talk to them about where Abby is?" Hagan asked.

"If they would tell the truth about things from back then," Ryan answered, "Because if they can provide names or places, it might help this investigation."

"True," Hagan said, "Though they might not be very willing to say much as they got paid for giving her up. They worked with these people multiple times."

"Might still be useful to ask," Ryan said.

"It might be," Hagan said.

"Did you get her social services record?" Ryan asked.

"I did," Hagan answered, "It gave an account of the accident along with a report from the school. It was also flagged."

"Flagged for what?" Ryan asked.

"It appears that the report from the school caused it to be flagged," Hagan answered, "But the exact reason or for who is not listed. But it wasn't done by the social worker; it was done by someone above her. To add strangeness to the whole situation, Selena had her file opened months before the accident while her brother's file was only opened a few days after the accident. The file also revealed her family tree, which showed that they didn't have any family to take them in."

"That does sound strange," Ryan said, "She shouldn't have been noticed by them unless her parents were dead or her parents were deemed unfit to care for her. Her and her brother would have both been looked at, so they would both have files."

"It was not in the file, but I suspect that her parent's deaths were not an accident," Hagan said, "It may also be my paranoia. Sometimes I see conspiracies where there are none."

"Someone was looking to take her from her parents and the only way to do it was to kill them," Ryan said, "That is concerning, especially given some recent events."

"It is," Hagan said, "But whoever we have been dealing with hasn't tried to kill us yet, so it may be a different department from the one who took her the first time. One might be the training department and the other is the one to put her to work."

"Either way, we need to figure out how to get the departments to talk to us," Ryan said.

"That is true," Hagan said, "Talking to the foster parents might be the ticket to getting to them. Although if the man is still out watching your apartment, he might be a better person to talk to about connecting with the departments."

"I really haven't looked out to see if he is still there," Ryan said, "With Tony staying on the couch, I haven't spent much time there. We can go look as long as we try not to wake Tony."

"Shouldn't be a problem," Hagan said. He and Ryan got up. They went into the living room. Tony was lying awkwardly on the couch and snoring. The two men moved as quietly as they could so not to wake Tony. The curtain was half over the window. They could peer around it without being seen from outside. Standing across the street where he had been standing before, was the man. It was the same man in the dark suit with the skinny tie.

"Looks government," Hagan said, "Not sure about any connection to Abigail."

"Best way to find out is to talk to him," Ryan said, "Without him leaving before we get a chance to."

"Is there a backdoor to this place?" Hagan asked.

"A fire exit the size of a window," Ryan answered.

"I'll go out there and you give me a few minutes to get around him before you come out to confront him," Hagan said.

"Okay," Ryan said, "This way to the fire exit."

Ryan led the way down the hallway to his office, which was the back bedroom. He opened the window and Hagan climbed out. Ryan closed it before going out to the living room again. Tony was still asleep. Ryan looked out the window and watched the man. The man moved his lips as if speaking to someone who was not there, but otherwise stood there glancing up at Ryan's apartment at regular intervals.

Ryan was starting to question whether enough time had passed for him to go out there when he saw Hagan leaning against a building farther down the street. He appeared to be waiting for Ryan. Without any further thoughts, Ryan went and got his shoes on. He went out the door and down to the sidewalk. Hagan saw him and started toward the man. Ryan checked the traffic before starting across the street. This move caused the man to notice Ryan. He did not move immediately but once Ryan was half-way across the street, the man started to back up a little bit.

Before the man could get far, he bumped into Hagan. Hagan held the man there as he pretended to apologize. Ryan finished crossing the street and reached them. He took the man's other arm and between him and Hagan moved the man up against the side of the building.

"What are you doing watching my place?" Ryan

asked.

"I don't know what you are talking about," the man answered.

"You have been standing out here several days and staring up at the window of my apartment," Ryan said, "The last time I tried to talk to you, you ran away. Those both suggest you know what I am talking about. So, who are you? Why are you watching my place? And who do you work for?"

"I work for the department of finance," the man answered.

"I did a consulting job for the finance department," Ryan said, "Why are you watching me?"

"There was some question about the security around the job," the man answered, "Especially after a media report came out a couple weeks ago that had information connected to it. So, I am supposed to be checking to see if it was you who leaked it."

"If you asked the man who recommended me, he would have told you the best way to deal with the situation is to knock on the door and ask me," Ryan said, "According to my agreement, which your boss had to have signed before I took the job, I do not contact the media without permission."

"Have you found any evidence as to who leaked the information to the media?" Hagan asked.

"My college has found evidence it was someone who was fired from our office not long ago," the man answered, "But I was ordered to continue my surveillance anyway."

"You know it isn't me, but you are continuing to watch me?" Ryan asked.

"You have never done something because you were

ordered to without it making sense?" the man said.

"How long until this is going away?" Ryan asked.

"Hopefully soon," the man answered.

"Have you noticed anything weird around?" Hagan asked.

"There were a couple of agents several days ago," the man answered, "But I don't know if they were connected to anything. The female who used to live in the apartment seems to have moved out and a man has since moved in, but he would visit at regular intervals before that. Not being sure what you consider weird it is hard to tell you specifics."

"The two agents," Ryan said.

"They showed up but didn't talk to me," the man said, "I'm not sure they noticed me. They didn't stay long; just two days. I have mostly been here during the day, but they were on twenty-four-hour surveillance. Then they were gone and they haven't shown back up."

"I'm gonna guess they were last seen three days ago," Hagan said.

"About that, yes," the man said, "Something specific about that day?"

"They broke in and left a present," Ryan answered, "Which might have caused you some problems with your boss. But that isn't a problem anymore."

"I am sensing there is more to that story," the man said.

"The female, as you referred to her, has been kidnapped," Ryan said, "And now someone is trying to stop me from searching for her."

"Who is it?" the man asked.

"We don't know," Hagan answered, "Do you know where the agents are from?"

"Unfortunately, I don't know," the man answered, "Due to there being several departments who use them."

"Any military?" Hagan asked.

"Most," the man answered, "Military and agents doesn't narrow it down at all. You would need to give me more to work with."

"Let's go back inside," Ryan said as a couple was stopping and digging out their phones. Ryan and Hagan let go of the man and the three of them headed across the street together. They went up to Ryan's apartment and settled in the kitchen.

"I am Keith Benson," the man said.

"I'm Hagan," Hagan said.

"So, what else do you have on these agents?" Keith asked.

"Abigail was kidnapped last week in the middle of the night and I didn't even notice despite being next to her in the bed," Ryan answered, "We have since learned that during the history she didn't talk about she was sold at the age of fourteen by her foster parents and disappeared. She must have escaped them and gone into hiding before they found her again."

"That does sound military," Keith said as he nodded, "But the exact department would be difficult to pinpoint as departments who kidnap and train children don't like to be identified. If they can be identified then they can be outed for what they do."

"Taking childhoods from children should be outed," Ryan said.

"I am not going to argue on that matter because I don't agree with doing that to anyone," Keith said, "But government departments don't talk to each other very well."

"That does make things difficult," Ryan said, "But any and all help is appreciated."

"I can watch from the window and point them out if they show up again," Keith said, "But I can't really look into it until I go back to the office later this afternoon."

"That is acceptable," Ryan said, "One of the chairs in the living room is placed where you can lookout. Tony is sleeping in there."

"I will try not to disturb him," Keith said. He got up and went into the living room.

"I will continue my line of inquiries," Hagan said.

"Thank you," Ryan said.

Hagan left the apartment. Ryan made himself a sandwich and then went back to his office to continue working.

CHAPTER SIX

Voices from the living room interrupted Ryan's work this time. It sounded a lot like Tony was worried. Ryan decided he should go and explain things before Tony did anything questionable. Going out to the living room, Ryan found Tony sitting up on the couch and looking at Keith. Tony looked at Ryan.

"What is going on?" Tony asked.

"This is Keith and he is keeping an eye out for a couple of agents he saw hanging around three days ago," Ryan answered, "It is fine."

"Okay," Tony said, "I think I will find somewhere else to be for the rest of the afternoon." Tony got up.

"See you later," Ryan said. Tony headed down the hallway. Then they heard the door to the bathroom close.

"I haven't seen them," Keith said, "But it is much more comfortable in here than standing out there."

"Let me know before you leave," Ryan said.

"I will," Keith said. The bathroom door opened again, but the noise of Tony moving around was headed for the apartment door. It opened and then closed. Ryan went back to his office and his work.

Ryan wandered into the kitchen about suppertime. Keith had gone home an hour before. He was surprised that Tony had not returned. Ryan did not worry about it as he started making supper. Looking through his cupboards, Ryan realized that he had not gone grocery shopping in a while. There was enough foodstuff to cook with, but it was not choice ingredients for the recipes. Ryan started into the prepping of ingredients and cooking of food.

Without meaning to Ryan found his thoughts went back to the last time he actually cooked a full meal. Abby had been craving a specific meal and she had started it, but burned her hand and he had taken over the cooking. She had sat there on a stool and they had talked as he cooked. It was one of those conversations where their topics changed as someone thought of a new topic. Sometimes it was light and they laughed; sometimes it was deep and thoughtful.

Abby had talked about someone she had known who had their week old child taken away from them because a nurse was sure the mother was on drugs. The frustrating part was that the nurse had only seen the mother and baby for two minutes from a distance while the mother was visiting the health centre for a mother and baby time. The mother had never been on drugs, she had just been tired because the baby's father had run at the first hint of he was going to be a father and none of the rest of the mother's family was willing to help her. It caused six months of stress for the mother and the loss of bonding time.

Then Abby talked about a couple where the guy had guessed that his girlfriend was pregnant before the girlfriend did. So, he planned a party to announce to the world, which turned out to be quite the surprise to many people. Fortunately, everyone was happy and when the baby was born, it was born into a happy home.

Ryan talked about a childhood friend who was sure he would never have children; though he liked children and was good with them. The first year of college the guy met a lady who was upgrading because she did not finish high school due to getting pregnant. He had met the lady's daughter and they bonded instantly. The lady had been dating another guy, but that guy had little to no interest in spending time with the girl. That relationship ended not long after as the lady figured out which was better for her family. The guy found a job he could do from home and became a stay-at-home step-dad. Then just as she was finishing up her upgrading, she found herself pregnant again. But that time she had his support to continue her education and he would look after the children. For a guy who never expected to have children had four the last time Ryan had heard, even if the first did not carry any of his DNA.

It had been a great hour Ryan had with Abby. He always found it easy to talk to her and he loved listening to her. Whether it was a conversation with her or her reading something to him, Ryan enjoyed it. Today as he cooked, he missed her so much his chest hurt. For the first time since she disappeared, Ryan wanted to sink to the floor and cry. However, he knew it was not productive to anything and the food would burn. He did not bother to try to stop the tears that came without his awareness.

Finally, the supper was cooked. Ryan wiped his face before sitting down to eat. When he was done, he put the leftovers away and cleaned up the kitchen. Instead of going back to work, Ryan went into the living room. He sat down in the chair by the window and stared out. For the first time, he wished for it to be raining to match his mood, but the sun was shining through the clouds. People were out enjoying, especially couples and families. It did not make him feel any better but he did not feel like moving either.

Ryan was not sure how long he had been sitting there but it was starting to get dark outside when he heard the door to his apartment open. Tony came into the living room and sat down on the couch. He watched Ryan for a moment.

"Are you okay?" Tony asked.

"I'm feeling a little blue at the moment," Ryan answered, "I had a large reminder that something big was missing from my life as I was cooking supper and it is taking a while to come out of it."

"Okay," Tony said, "Did Hagan find something useful?"

"He had more on Abby's history and a possible way forward," Ryan answered, "How was the rest of your day?"

"I went to visit Audrey," Tony answered.

"How did that go?" Ryan asked.

"It actually went well," Tony answered, "Our relationship isn't fixed or perfect, or any of those other things people claim a relationship should be, but she is willing to let me move back in."

"That is great news," Ryan said, "And I am not saying that just because you have been crashing on my couch. You do better when you spending time around Audrey."

"Good to know," Tony said, "Because I have learned the same thing through the therapy sessions. As much as I always assumed I would find someone to be with and we would have a family, if I am better around Audrey and we can't have children then that is what is."

"There are other options if you want children," Ryan said, "They may not be biologically yours but you can love them like they are."

"I'm not sure Audrey and I are ready to talk about those options right now," Tony said, "That is a topic for some time down the road."

"True," Ryan said.

"Instead, we are focusing on where we are right now," Tony said, "Not on what we want, or pressuring each other to do things, but on our current situation."

"Well, I really hope it goes well for both of you," Ryan said.

"You sure you are going to be okay?" Tony asked.

"I will be," Ryan answered, "I will do everything I can to find Abby and if it doesn't work out, I will figure out what to do from there. But I really hope I find Abby."

"If she has been taken by the government, what are you going to do about it?" Tony asked, "You can't just demand your girlfriend back."

"You don't know until you have tried," Ryan said.

"You are going to make me come and check on you, aren't you?" Tony asked.

"I don't want to interrupt your time with Audrey," Ryan answered, "Hagan will be by to check on me."

"But he is adding to the crazy, not helping you out of it," Tony said.

"Right now, I don't want out of it," Ryan said, "I want to find Abby, even if I have to fight the government to have access to her."

"You know that sounds insane, right?" Tony asked.

"I do," Ryan answered, "Would you abandon Audrey just because there are some obstacles between you and her?"

"Probably not," Tony answered, "I just don't want to lose a friend over this all."

"I am not going to lie and say everything will be okay," Ryan said, "But I am not giving up on Abby."

"I suppose it would be an impossible ask," Tony said.

"It would be the same as me asking you to give up Audrey," Ryan said, "I would never ask that of you."

Tony nodded. He looked like he wanted to add things and what Ryan was telling him prevented it. Ryan thought about offering up more but decided if his words had not convinced Tony than nothing more he said would. Hagan had tried to explain that to Ryan the other day and now Ryan understood it.

"So, what now?" Tony asked.

"You go home and enjoy your time with Audrey," Ryan answered, "I go to bed alone and tomorrow I got back to what I have been trying to do since Abby disappeared. I'm not sure what else you mean."

"I guess that is the answer," Tony said, "I just feel like I am saying goodbye to a good friend."

"You can come back to visit," Ryan said, "I am not

gone yet. We haven't gotten far enough in the investigation to go anywhere."

"Yeah," Tony said. He got to his feet. Ryan watched Tony leave the living room. As he heard Tony lock the door, Ryan wondered if he should have gotten his key back. He shrugged it off as he trusted Tony with the key. The worst likely to happen was finding Tony back on his couch.

Ryan looked out the window again. It was dark out there now and the light was coming from the street lights. People were still going by as they went about their business, whether heading out for an evening or heading home for the night. Going about their normal lives, which caused Ryan to miss Abby and the evenings spent sitting on the couch with her. Thinking about her made Ryan think about people watching his apartment. He tried to see what was between street lights but he was not good at it.

Having sat there for another couple hours, Ryan found his eyes drifting close instead of watching the street. If someone was watching, they were not out there now. Ryan got up and headed off to bed.

When Hagan knocked on the apartment door, Ryan was sitting in the kitchen with a cup of coffee and a bowl of cereal. Ryan let Hagan in and they went back to the kitchen.

"Where is your friend today?" Hagan asked.

"He went back to his girlfriend," Ryan answered, "Keith out there again today?"

"I didn't see him," Hagan answered, "But it is still early in the day. If he was out there, I would have asked if he had any answers for us."

"Maybe he will have some answers later," Ryan said, "We will have to wait and see."

"True," Hagan said, "I really don't have any more answers than yesterday, but I have been thinking. Our best shot at getting answers might be to talk to the foster parents and get answers out of them, or if that isn't possible then contact information for the agency they gave Selena to."

"We will have to find something we can use to gain the information from them," Ryan said, "Because they aren't likely to give the information without something."

"I have been doing some digging and I have some stuff we can blackmail them with, if it becomes necessary," Hagan said.

"I would feel bad for doing such things to them," Ryan said, "But they haven't shown any reason to feel guilty about the matter. Do you need me to book the tickets?"

"It would help a lot," Hagan said.

"What time would be best to get there?" Ryan asked, "And how long do you think we will need to be there?"

"Probably just one morning," Hagan answered, "It is better for the morning when any foster children will be at school as I don't think we want to involve them in this."

"That makes sense," Ryan said. After a sip of coffee, Ryan got up and went to his office. He brought back his laptop and booted it up. It did not take him long to get to the airline website. Hagan looked over his shoulder as Ryan worked. Ryan found a flight for early the next morning with two seats available and a return flight set for early evening.

"I hope you aren't expecting first class," Ryan said.

"I don't expect first class," Hagan said, "Most of my clients wouldn't want to come and thus would only pay for the flight in the final bill rather than buy a ticket."

"That is how one finds very cheap flights," Ryan said.

"It is," Hagan said.

"I will print off the ticket for you," Ryan said.

"Thank you," Hagan said.

Ryan got up and went to his office where the ticket was waiting on the printer. He returned with it to the kitchen and gave it to Hagan. Hagan nodded as he accepted it.

"Then I will see you tomorrow at the crack of dawn," Hagan said as he got to his feet.

"Sorry but there wasn't an earlier flight," Ryan said. Hagan chuckled. Ryan walked him to the door. Hagan left and Ryan locked up behind him. Then Ryan went back to the kitchen. He got his laptop and took it into the living room. Sitting down in the chair, he worked as he occasionally looked out the window. He did not see Keith, but he also did not see any other agents or anyone suspicious.

Ryan was so absorbed in his work that the knock at the door caused him to jump a little. He put the laptop on the coffee table before going to the door. Ryan checked through the peephole and saw his usual mailman. He opened the door.

"Good day," the mailman said holding out a clipboard, "Just need your signature."

"Of course," Ryan said. He signed the paper where indicated.

"Thank you," the mailman said before handing over a letter, "Have a good day."

"You too," Ryan said. The mailman left and Ryan withdrew into his apartment. He locked the door before examining the letter. It was marked registered mail and has his address, but there was no return address. Ryan carefully felt the envelope. It was a standard business envelope and the only thing he felt was paper. He wondered if it was safe to open, but his curiosity got the better of him and Ryan opened it.

The only thing inside was a sheet of paper folded into three. Ryan shook it open and read it.

Dear Ryan,

I am sorry I did not leave a note, but I was distracted by my own mind. I left because I needed some space. Please do not look for me. I am fine.

Abigail.

Ryan read it over again and shook his head. The handwriting was similar to Abby's, however, it lacked some of the swirls he was used to seeing. Also, the wording was not right and it was not just the clinical tone. Ryan was not sure who thought this would work, but it was likely whoever decided to turn up after someone called Abby's cellphone. It was like the people who took her did and didn't understand how to be covert. Maybe Hagan was right about the military connection. It did sound like the joke about military intelligence Ryan had heard.

Ryan took the letter to his office and placed it in a file folder along with the envelope. He closed it and put it away in his filing cabinet. Then he went back to the living room. Keeping himself behind the curtain, Ryan looked out the window. However, he still did not see any agents or anyone suspicious. But then if they thought the letter worked, they would think he would stop his search.

With a shrug, Ryan sat down in the chair again and went back to work. He tried to keep an eye on what was happening out the window, but easily got sucked into his work.

Ryan was once again lost in his work when a knock at the door interrupted him. He got up and went to the door. This time it was Audrey he saw through the peephole. He opened the door.

"Hello," Ryan said.

"Hi," Audrey said, "I was worrying if I could ask you about something."

"Sure," Ryan said, "Come in."

Audrey stepped inside and Ryan closed the door. They went into the living room and sat down.

"What's up?" Ryan asked.

"Tony has been acting worried and when I ask him he won't tell me," Audrey answered, "I was wondering if you knew what was wrong."

"He is worried that my current project could end up with me dead," Ryan said.

"I know you consult on all sorts of things, but dead?" Audrey asked.

"It is a personal project," Ryan answered.

"What kind of project would you being doing that might be dangerous?" Audrey asked, "You never seemed to be the type of person."

"Normally, I wouldn't be into dangerous situations," Ryan answered, "But this project is different."

"How does Abigail feel about you and this project?"

Audrey asked.

"It is unlikely she knows about it," Ryan answered.

"What do you mean?" Audrey asked, "Why wouldn't she know?"

"Because finding her is the project," Ryan answered.

"If she left, maybe she doesn't want to be found," Audrey said.

"I considered that," Ryan said, "And if I thought she had left because she wanted to, I wouldn't be searching for her. However, I have already seen the video of the men leaving with her and I hardly think she went with them willingly."

"I can see why that would be dangerous," Audrey said, "Are you sure about it?"

"Yes," Ryan answered, "The answers I have found since suggest she was kidnapped and it is dangerous. I didn't mind Tony staying on my couch for a while because it meant someone else was around."

"He can come back and stay for a while if you need," Audrey said.

"No, it is better for him to be with you," Ryan said, "He would just keep trying to talk me out of my project."

"Of course he would," Audrey said, "Unfortunately, he gives up on some things far too easily."

"If he doesn't have a vested interest or an emotional connection, any obstacle is too big," Ryan said, "I understand that and I tried to convince him that me looking for Abigail would be like him looking for you if you disappeared. He still tried to keep convincing me to give up."

"Then you are right about him staying with me," Audrey said.

"I think at this point it doesn't matter if anyone else is here or not," Ryan said.

"I will get Tony to check on you occasionally," Audrey said.

"That is fine," Ryan said, "Everything between you two going to okay?"

"I'm encouraging Tony to keep going to the therapist," Audrey said, "I think it is helping him come to terms with our situation. I think we might survive it."

'That is good," Ryan said, "Did you tell Abigail about losing the baby?"

"I might have," Audrey answered.

"Might have?" Ryan asked.

"She and Savanna had taken me out shortly afterward," Audrey answered, "We have some drinks and I don't necessarily remember everything we talked about. It was strongly on my mind. Why are you asking?"

"I just remember her talking about people who had children and babies," Ryan answered, "And I was wondering if she was thinking about your situation and that led her thinking about other situations with babies."

"You don't think she was pregnant?" Audrey asked.

"If she was, she was drinking during," Ryan answered, "We shared a couple drinks less than twenty-four hours before she disappeared."

"She wouldn't do that," Audrey said, "I may not know her very well, but I do know that. Maybe she was talking about it to gauge your thoughts on having children."

"She may have been doing that," Ryan said, "I just remembered the conversation and wondered. I have been focusing more on finding her."

"I hope you do," Audrey said, "She is a great person. Are you getting close to finding her?"

"I don't really know," Ryan said, "But I keep hoping."

"I should get back," Audrey said as she stood up, "Tony went off to his therapy session for the day and is due back soon."

"You didn't tell him you were coming here?" Ryan asked as he got up as well.

"He refused to tell me why he was so worried and he seemed to think it shouldn't matter," Audrey answered as they walked towards the door.

"He should know better," Ryan said.

"He should," Audrey said.

"Good luck with him," Ryan said as he opened the apartment door.

"Thanks," Audrey said with a tight smile before leaving.

Ryan closed the door and locked it behind her. Rather than going back to the living room, Ryan went into the kitchen to warm up some leftovers to eat.

After eating, Ryan had gone back to working for a while. He could focus for a time, but then his concentration was gone. Ryan looked out the window for a short while and it made him feel isolated. While putting his laptop back in his office to get away from the window and the feeling, Ryan decided to go for a walk. It had not rained all day, so Ryan put his shoes on, grabbed his keys along with his wallet, and locked the door behind him.

It was a lovely evening. The clouds were not as dark as they had been. Ryan found himself okay with the temperature outside. There were couples out for a walk as well as people who were moving with more purpose. Seeing the couples made Ryan miss Abby and he tried not to pay attention to them.

Ryan got as far as the Tavern. The door opened as a couple came out and invited him inside. Ryan sat down at the bar.

"Haven't seen you in a while," Lucas said, "Beer?"

"Please," Ryan answered.

"Your perfect ten return?" Lucas asked as he poured a beer.

"No," Ryan answered.

"I am sorry," Lucas said as he set the beer in front of Ryan, "Throwing yourself into work?"

"Jey and Savanna keep inviting me to clubs to listen to Smash," Ryan answered before taking a sip of the beer.

"I can't imagine being around Savanna would help with the breakup," Lucas said, "But I suppose listening to the music does."

"Somewhat," Ryan said, "Going without Abigail doesn't make things easier as I am used to going with her."

"Yeah, that does make it harder," Lucas said with a nod, "Tony hasn't been around much either."

"He has spent the last while staying on my couch," Ryan said, "He has been going to therapy to try and fix his relationship with his girlfriend."

"Has it actually helped him?" Lucas asked, "Because he doesn't really seem the type."

"She says it has," Ryan answered, "But he is still has a lot of work to go."

"Of course," Lucas said. Someone farther down the

bar called for service. Lucas went down to serve them. Ryan drank from the beer. He was half-finished it before Lucas wandered back.

"So, back to get blind drunk and forget your troubles?" Lucas asked.

"I have a plane to catch in the morning," Ryan answered, "Otherwise, I would."

"Where are you going?" Lucas asked.

"I have a project that requires it," Ryan answered.

"Maybe you should take some personal time while you are out of town and away from all your memories," Lucas said, "I know you are unlikely to find another perfect ten, but maybe you find someone who can help you move on."

"Sounds like a solid and logical plan," Ryan said.

"You aren't going to take it, are you?" Lucas asked.

"It is nothing against your advice or you," Ryan answered, "It is good advice and I would probably suggest it for people in my situation. I'm just not sure that I am ready to follow it."

"Understandable," Lucas said, "And nice to know I haven't lost my ability to give advice."

"How about another beer to make me feel better on the matter?" Ryan asked.

"Sure," Lucas answered, "It always makes me feel better to pour beer." He poured another beer and set it in front of Ryan.

"Then you have the right job for you," Ryan said.

Lucas smiled before going down the bar to tend to someone else. Ryan sipped the beer. A group at the end of the bar was having party and they were paying for multiple shots per person, which meant Lucas was stuck there for a while. Ryan did not mind as he sipped his beer. Ryan's beer was finished by the time Lucas made it back.

"Another?" Lucas asked.

"No, I think that is it for this evening," Ryan answered.

"Are you going to be okay?" Lucas asked as Ryan took out the cash to pay for his beers and a tip for Lucas.

"I hope so," Ryan said.

"Have a good night," Lucas said.

"You too," Ryan said. He left the Tavern and headed back towards his apartment. Once he was in sight of the apartment, Ryan stopped and looked up and down the street. It was starting to get dark, but the street lights had not come on yet. As with the rest of the day, Ryan did not see anyone. He had not even seen Keith.

Ryan was starting to feel he was getting paranoid. He had been cautious about things before this matter. Now he felt like he was being watched all the time and he expected it. He wondered if Abigail felt like that while she was living with him. The information Hagan had gotten about her cellphone and her new identity suggested she worked hard to avoid that feeling. Someone had been helping her do those things because someone had called her once to inform her of danger. Hagan had never gotten the name of who had been on the other end of the phone, but Ryan was not worried about it at this point. The person might have intentionally made it hard to figure who they were as the flashes of competence suggested it took work to stay out of sight.

It was better to not give up the person by accident when all Ryan wanted was to find Abigail. Ryan did wonder why the person had not warned Abigail this time. Maybe they had already been caught, or they did not know to be able to do so. If they were not able to warn her, it was worrying for Ryan. There were many things he was worried about and they were crowding his mind.

Ryan started walking again. He had never thought he would end up in any situation like this. Not that he had a specific plan for his life, but this was a sharp turn from what he expected. All he had wanted was his girlfriend back. That was all he wanted this whole time. Somehow he doubted they would give her back if he asked. Now he was too far to give up and he did not want to do that.

Reaching his apartment, Ryan unlocked the door and went inside. He locked the door behind him. The paranoia was back and caused Ryan to wander the apartment to see if there were any traces of someone else having been there. He did not see, smell, or feel anything different. Then he shrugged to himself. It was not like he was going to be doing anything other than sleeping.

Ryan got ready for bed and crawled in. He hoped the alcohol would be enough to let him sleep. However, his eyes would not close and he kept seeing the empty side of the bed. Getting up, Ryan went to the living room. He lay down on the couch. It did not take long for him to drift off.

CHAPTER SEVEN

When the taxi dropped Ryan off at the airport, he found
Hagan already waiting for him. Hagan had a backpack
with him. They walked together to the counter to check-
in.

"Not bringing anything with you?" Hagan asked.

"I have everything I need," Ryan answered.

"You have never been stuck somewhere without a
way home?" Hagan asked.

"No, I haven't," Ryan answered, "Also, even if I did,
I know I can buy anything I might need. I also don't
travel much."

Hagan nodded. There was not much of a line at the
counter and Hagan was helped first. Ryan stepped up to
the counter once Hagan moved aside. The lady behind
the counter was effective at her job and Ryan joined
Hagan on the walk to the boarding area. Something at
the corner of Ryan's eye caught his eye and he turned
his head slightly. There was a man in a suit, who

appeared to be an agent of some sort, was standing next to the entrance.

"He arrived in the taxi behind you," Hagan said.

"Apparently, I am too tired to notice before now," Ryan said.

"After all this, you are paying more attention?" Hagan asked.

"I have been," Ryan answered, "But I didn't sleep well last night and today I'm tired."

"Are you going to be ready to deal with Selena's foster parents?" Hagan asked.

"I'll sleep on the plane and be better when we get there," Ryan answered.

"I have never been good at sleeping on anything moving," Hagan said, "But if you can and feel okay afterward, good for you. I have a book to help me."

"Should be a quiet flight then," Ryan said, "I doubt the man in the suit will be on the same flight."

"They could have figured out which flight we are on and gotten a ticket for him," Hagan said, "They had the time."

"I guess we will see," Ryan said, "He will be in a rush if he wants on."

"True," Hagan said.

They reached the security area. Hagan went through security first and Ryan followed. They barely got through before the call for boarding their flight came over the loudspeaker. Ryan did not watch for the man in the suit as they lined up for boarding, however, he noticed Hagan keeping an eye out.

They boarded the plane. Hagan got the middle seat and Ryan was on the aisle. As everyone else coming in and sitting down. They did not see the man in the suit.

Finally, the door of the plane was closed.

"I guess he didn't get a ticket," Hagan said, "That should be good for us as I am slightly worried that they would try to stop us from having our discussion with the foster parents."

"As long as they are not there already waiting for us," Ryan said.

"That would be my thought as well," Hagan said, "But I would have thought they would have bought a ticket just in case."

"Maybe he was just outside my apartment this morning and followed me when I left without knowing where I was headed."

"I hope so," Hagan said, "It will be better for us."

"It would," Ryan said and then found himself yawning. Hagan took out his book. Ryan did not bother to look at the title; instead, he closed his eyes and was soon drifting off to sleep.

Something bumped Ryan in the side waking him up. He opened his eyes and looked around. It appeared that the plane had landed and people were gathering their stuff. Hagan was looking at him expectantly and Ryan realized what bumped him was Hagan's elbow. Ryan got up and stretched before following everyone else off the plane.

On the sidewalk out front of the airport, Ryan and Hagan caught a taxi. Hagan gave the driver the address. Ryan let Hagan and the taxi driver talk. They talked about the weather and world news. Hagan was vague about where he and Ryan were from, but the driver did not notice or was used to such answers.

The taxi stopped in front of the house. The driver

looked at it for a long moment, but he did not say anything more than the amount owed. Ryan paid it and then he and Hagan got out. The taxi left.

"He knows something he didn't tell us," Hagan said.

"The last taxi driver knew the Warners and he told about them," Ryan said as he went through the gate.

"Do all the taxi drivers know about them?" Hagan asked.

"Maybe if they have a connection to child services," Ryan answered.

"That is concerning," Hagan said.

Ryan knocked on the door. He nodded. They waited several minutes before the door opened. The woman who claimed to be Lindsay Wilson stood there.

"What do you want?" she asked Ryan, "I told you last time I was not the person you were looking for."

"I know you did, Mrs. Wilson," Ryan replied, "We just want to talk to you about a child who was in your care."

She looked at Ryan for a long minute and then at Hagan. Ryan sensed that she was really not sure about letting them inside.

"I'm sure we will only take a few minutes of your time, madam," Hagan said with a smile. He looked friendly with a smile. This apparently was enough for her and she stepped out of the way to let them come inside.

"Tea?" she asked.

"Sounds wonderful," Hagan answered.

"You will have to excuse the mess," she said as she led the way to the kitchen.

"It is understandable," Hagan said.

Ryan looked into the living room as they went

passed and saw that it looked like several children of various ages lived there.

"I'm guessing you currently have children who are school-aged," Hagan said.

"My husband and I don't take on children who aren't school-aged," she replied, "I feel too old to manage children who are younger."

They reached the kitchen. Ryan and Hagan sat down at the kitchen table while she moved around getting the tea ready.

"How do you enjoy being a foster parent?" Hagan asked.

"It is a good feeling and the children are wonderful," she answered, "Some are troubled, but that is okay. It just means they need some attention and someone to listen."

The kettle must have been boiled recently because it did not take long to boil again. She poured the water into a teapot before bringing the teapot and cups to the table. After pouring a cup for each of them, she sat down at the table with them.

"Anyway, there is only so much I can tell you about any child who has been in my care due to privacy issues," she said, "If I can remember the child. Some children don't stay long enough for them to make an impact due to their situation."

"Oh, I am sure you have a fine memory," Hagan said, "She was in the system for three years and in your care for much of that time."

"What is her name?" she asked.

"At the time, she was called Selena Stafferson," Hagan answered.

"I think you are confused," she said, "I don't

remember having a child by that name under my care."

"According to the records I found, you did," Hagan said taking a file out of his backpack and opened it as if looking for the information, "Back when you went by the name Liza Warner, you had Selena under your care until you sold her to the Platt Truman School for Exceptional Students."

"I am not sure what you are talking about," she said. A concerned look came over her face and Ryan guessed she was regretting letting them in.

"Nine years ago you changed your name to Lindsay Wilson after you and your husband were accused of abuse after a child under your care, correct?" Hagan asked.

"I am Lindsay Wilson and I have always been Lindsay Wilson," she answered, "I am not sure why you would have this false information."

Hagan did not say anything immediately. Instead, he laid a picture on the table. It was a native boy with bruises on the side of his face and an arm in a cast.

"You are saying you don't remember being Liza Warner who watched your husband abuse this boy, Aspen George?" Hagan asked.

"I just told you that is not me," she said.

"I wonder if social services would be interested in seeing if there is a connection between you and Liza Warner," Hagan said. He put another photo on the table. This one was of her and a man but it was definitely several years old. "On the other hand, you talk to us about Selena Stafferson and any connection they make will not be through us."

She stared at the photo for a long time as Hagan and Ryan waited for her answer. It was a long time before she looked up at Hagan with a scared look in her eyes.

"I don't have any answers for you," she said.

"If we didn't think you had the answer we wanted, we would not be here talking to you," Hagan said.

What do you want to know?" she asked. Her voice sounded defeated.

"We need the information about who you contacted to send Selena odd to the school," Hagan answered.

"They just gave me a phone number," she said.

"Then provide us with the phone number," Hagan said.

She got up and went over to the area where there was a phone attached to the wall. On the counter under was a container, which she opened. Inside were cards. She went through them until she found the card she was looking for and took it out before returning to the table.

"It doesn't work all the time," she said.

"We aren't worried about that," Hagan said, "This is the information we are looking for." He took the photos off the table and put them back in the file. Hagan put the file away before taking the card.

"How do I know you will not tell people about the rest of it?" she asked as she gestured toward his bag.

"You will just have to trust us," Hagan answered, "Thank you for the tea."

Ryan and Hagan stood up. They left her sitting there and went out the front door closing it behind them. Going down the path, they exited the yard and headed to the left.

"You don't seem surprised over my methods of extracting information," Hagan said.

"The only reason I would have objected is if you used violence," Ryan said, "I am too far into this to start objecting to threatening people, especially when we wouldn't get what we want any other way."

"Good to know," Hagan said, "Let's see what this number does." Hagan took out his cellphone. He put it on speakerphone before dialling the number from the card. It rang and rang and rang. There was no voicemail or answering machine or anything else to answer in the place of a human. Hagan waited even when Ryan felt like it was too long.

"No one seems to be home, just Mrs. Warner said," Hagan said when he finally ended the call. But it did not stop him from hitting redial. Once again, it rang and was not answered.

"Might only be answered when they are expecting someone to call," Ryan said.

"I will keep trying anyway," Hagan said as he ended the call. He took it off speakerphone before putting his cell away.

"We should call a taxi to get back to the airport," Ryan said, "Unless there is somewhere else you think we should go."

"I don't have any," Hagan answered, "But finding a place to eat sounds good."

"There is a great restaurant out at the airport," Ryan said.

"Good," Hagan said. He took his phone back out and called a taxi. They had reached the corner and stopped. Ryan leaned against the light pole as they waited. It was ten minutes before the taxi arrived. Ryan and Hagan got in. Hagan asked for them to be taken to the airport. Once again, Hagan talked with the driver while Ryan was quiet.

When they arrived, Ryan paid the fare before they

got out. Before the taxi could leave, someone else waved it down. Ryan led the way into the airport. In the opposite direction from the counters and security were a restaurant and gift shop. It was a sit-down restaurant with a sign at the entrance that they should wait to be seated. The hostess came a moment later and she confirmed how many before leading them to a seat near a window between the restaurant and the airport. She left them with the menus and promise their server would be right with them.

While they were browsing the menu, Hagan used his phone to call the number again. He must not have gotten an answer because he ended the call and put his phone away. It was then that their server arrived. He took their drink order before leaving them alone. When he brought their drinks, he took their order.

"We haven't been followed since we got here," Hagan said, "So, you were likely correct in your idea that they followed you when you left your apartment this morning. I would suggest you be watchful when you return because they may use your absence to make another attempt to distract you."

"I will be careful," Ryan said.

"I suggest a CO2 detector," Hagan said.

"I would have to stop and buy one," Ryan said.

"You can usually find one at hardware stores, some department stores, or grocery stores," Hagan said.

"I can stop at one on the way home," Ryan said, "I haven't gotten around to grocery shopping in a while, so I should do that anyway. I just wasn't originally planning to do it today."

"I thought it might be a good idea to mention it to avoid you getting sick again," Hagan said, "I am not as worried about it because someone else is staying at my place as well as where I am staying. I would worry less but your friend went home."

"He needed to go," Ryan said, "And I will be okay. I will invest in a CO2 detector and inspect my place before relaxing."

"Good," Hagan said, "I will keep calling this number and then stop tomorrow to see if Keith is back."

"If he has some answers, it would be nice," Ryan said.

"Hopefully," Hagan said.

The server brought their food and made sure they were all right before leaving them to eat. They started eating and skipped talking.

When they were finished eating, Ryan paid the bill and they left the restaurant. He and Hagan went to check-in for the flight. There was nothing unusual or caught their attention. On the occasions he could, Hagan had his cellphone to his ear; but he turned it to airplane mode before they boarded. Hagan went back to his book and Ryan let himself drift off to sleep.

The shift caused by the lane descending woke Ryan this time and by the time the plane had landed, he was fully awake. Hagan did not put his book away until just before people were let off the plane. They went along with everyone else for the first part, but when most moved toward the luggage claim area, they went towards the exit.

"I have a ride from here," Hagan said.

"See you tomorrow," Ryan said.

"Be careful," Hagan said.

"You too," Ryan said. Hagan headed for the parking

lot while Ryan stayed on the curb. He looked around for a taxi he could hire. Out of the corner of his eye, Ryan saw the man in the suit leaning against the wall farther down. The man in the suit had already noticed Ryan. Ryan continued a few steps forward to the first taxi in the line.

"Good evening, sir," the driver greeted Ryan, "Any luggage?"

"Not today," Ryan answered. The driver held the door for Ryan before going around to get into the driver's seat.

"Where to?" the driver asked.

Ryan gave the address for the club Smash usually played at.

"Very good, sir," the driver said. He then pulled away from the curb and concentrated on driving. Ryan tried not to check through the back window to see if the taxi was being followed. The driver did not try to make conversation. Occasionally Ryan could hear him humming quietly to himself.

Half-way to the club, the driver quit humming and started checking his mirrors more frequently. Ryan did not look back because he was pretty sure he knew that the man in the suit was following them and that was what he would see.

"May I ask you a question, sir?" the driver asked.

"Sure," Ryan answered.

"Do you work for the government security, sir?" the driver asked.

"Are you asking if I am a spy?" Ryan asked.

"Well, sir, you came out of the airport without luggage, you request a public place to be dropped off, and we are being followed by a man in a dark coloured car," the driver said.

"I suppose that would make sense," Ryan said, "But no, I am not a spy. I'm a consultant who has taken on a job that seems to have attracted unexpected interest."

"Ah, I see," the driver said but in a tone suggesting he did not quite believe Ryan, "Would you like me to lose the person following, sir?"

"Thank you for the offer," Ryan said, "But I don't feel it is necessary."

"Very well, sir," the driver said. He quit checking his mirrors as frequently as he was no longer worried about the vehicle following them.

They arrived at the club and the driver pulled up to the curb.

"Are you sure, sir?" the driver asked turning to look at Ryan.

"I will be fine," Ryan answered. He offered the driver the amount for the fare as well as a good tip.

"Very well, sir," the driver said taking the money, "Good luck to you."

"Thank you," Ryan said before getting out. He closed the door before going to the door. The bouncer accepted the cover and let him inside. Entering the club, the band Ryan could hear was not Smash. They were not bad. Ryan looked over the crowd and saw Savanna sitting by herself at a booth. Ryan made his way through the crowd to sit down opposite her.

"I didn't expect you to come," Savanna said, "Jey said he couldn't reach you. Did you get his message?"

"No, I have been out of town most of the day," Ryan said, "But since I found myself being followed, I thought I would stop in."

"You thought coming here would be a good idea

when you are being followed?" Savanna asked.

"Because that was what came to my mind," Ryan answered, "It doesn't really matter overall as he has been following me since I left my apartment this morning."

"Well, I am sure Jey will be happy to see you here," Savanna said.

"Should I ask why?" Ryan asked.

"I don't really know," Savanna answered, "He just got excited and then tried to call you. Before I could ask, he got distracted and I didn't get to ask."

"Then I will have to wait," Ryan said.

"The band isn't going to be sticking around very long after the show," Savanna said, "They have to go home and get some sleep because they are leaving town tomorrow morning."

"Their manager got them to agree to get up before noon?" Ryan asked, "How?"

"He promised they could sleep on the bus," Savanna answered, "Also breakfast. And money."

"Fame too?"

"He keeps trying that one whenever they ask why they should do anything he suggests, though he also uses money quite frequently. This was the first time he used the promise of sleep and food."

"Didn't Jey say they were recording the album before starting to tour?"

"That was the plan among Jey and the rest of the band, but their new manager has other plans and this is the first time he has managed to sway them to his plan."

"How far are they going?"

"They are going to be part of a festival. I don't know much more than that. Girlfriends aren't invited."

"Not enough seats on the bus?"

"I don't know."

The band finished their set and left the stage. They were replaced by the club manager, who was there to announce Smash. The server stopped by the table to refresh Savanna's drink and let Ryan order one. He noticed that Savanna was not drinking alcohol, but it did not stop him from ordering a drink with alcohol. The band came on and started into their set. Ryan settled in to enjoy the show. Savanna did the same. Tonight Oscar did not join them.

It was a good performance. They played a few new songs. Ryan thought they were just as good as the old ones. Savanna was enjoying herself, but there was some worry in her fidgeting. Ryan was not letting anything worry him, even the feeling and knowledge that the man in the suit was watching him.

When Smash finished their performance, the server stopped at their table to offer refills but Savanna refused. Ryan offered the money for the bill, which the server accepted before going off. Once the server had moved on, Savanna got up. Ryan followed her as she headed backstage. The bouncer at the door preventing people from going back there let them through. It was darker back there but Savanna knew her way. The band was relaxing and unwinding.

"You got my message," Jey said as he jumped up, "I really hoped you would."

"I'm here, but I can't say I got your message," Ryan said. Jey looked confused for a moment and the shrugged.

"I got a phone call this afternoon," Jey said, "And I couldn't wait to tell you the news."

"Okay," Ryan said.

"Dennis called!" Jey bounced at his statement. Ryan paused as he tried to remember who Dennis was. Then it came to him and Ryan smiled.

"He actually called?" Ryan asked, "I didn't think he would."

"I never thought you were anywhere close to serious when you told me about him," Jey said, "But then he called."

"Who is Dennis?" Savanna asked. The rest of the band seemed just as confused.

"A few months back I got a job from one of those guys who knows a guy and he was happy with my work," Ryan said, "He thought I did a good enough job that he wanted to do me a favour. I couldn't think of anything at the time, so I suggest he could get Dennis Stark to call Jey."

"The Dennis Stark?" Chase asked, "Made famous by his time with the Yeahmen and has been known to help bands become just as famous? Why didn't you tell us this earlier?"

"I wanted to tell Ryan first," Jey answered, "After he got me the phone call."

"So, what did Dennis say?" Ryan asked.

"He is going to be at the festival and he couldn't wait to hear us play," Jey said. The whole band whooped. Ryan smiled and Savanna hugged Jey.

"Congratulations," Ryan said, "I hope this meeting with Dennis goes excellent."

"I wish I got to go with you," Savanna said.

"If we are meeting Dennis, we can't go alone," the keyboardist said, "If I get to meet Dennis without Lacy, she will never talk to me again. I would not even get to meet my unborn child."

"A judge would rule for joint custody," Chase said, "So, I wouldn't worry too much."

"Thanks, buddy," the keyboardist's tone was dry.

"Why aren't you taking girlfriends to this festival?" Ryan asked.

"Our manager said so," Chase answered, "We asked when we found out we were busing to the festival, since it wouldn't cost any more than it already was."

"I think we may have to show up in pairs tomorrow morning," Jey said, "Because there is no reason to leave people behind."

"He is going to argue," Chase said.

"He has argued with everything we have done so far," Jey said with a shrug, "What is new about that?"

"True," Chase answered, "Though he is paying for this trip, so he might push back a little more."

"He is going to be introduced to Dennis Stark," the keyboardist said, "I think he can give in this time without issue."

"True," Jey said.

"We should get Oscar to give Ryan a ride home," Savanna said, "He said he was being followed."

"Shouldn't be a problem," Jey said, "I am so glad you came tonight." Jey grabbed Ryan and pulled him into a hug. Ryan hugged him back and expected Jey to let him go. Instead, Jey squeezed him tighter.

"Breathing," Ryan gasped.

"We will never be able to repay you for getting Dennis Stark to show interest in us," Jey said. He let up. Ryan was able to free an arm and pat Jey on the back.

"I'm sure I might be able to think of something someday," Ryan said.

"You will have to come to our next show," Chase said, "So that we can tell you all about the festival."

"I look forward to that," Ryan said as he patted Jey on the back again. Finally, Jey let go.

Oscar came into the room. Everyone looked at him. He looked back and appeared to be confused by everyone standing around. Then Oscar shrugged and left the room.

"He was probably coming in to see if we were packed up and ready to go," Jey said, "Let's go."

The band members started to pack up and Ryan helped them. By the time Oscar came back, they were ready to leave.

Ryan was dropped off first. He stopped outside the door and looked around. He did not see the man in the suit, nor did he see anyone else who appeared suspicious. A check of the door showed no sign of foreign entry. Ryan unlocked the door and went inside. He walked through the whole apartment twice making sure nothing was out of the ordinary and there was no sign of anyone else having in the apartment. In his bedroom, Ryan opened his window a small amount. When he felt comfortable, Ryan got ready and went to bed.

CHAPTER EIGHT

The coffee machine was just finished when there was a knock at the apartment door. Ryan put down his mug before going to answer it. Hagan was standing there. Ryan let him in before leading the way to the kitchen. Picking up his mug again, Ryan filled it with coffee. He was about to put it back when he stopped and offered it to Hagan.

"I'm fine," Hagan said. Ryan nodded and then put the coffee pot back on the machine. Then he sat down on a stool with his mug. Ryan took a sip before turning his attention to Hagan.

"Anything?" Ryan asked.

"Unfortunately, no," Hagan answered, "I have been calling the number and haven't had any response. I was hoping that if we annoyed them enough that they would contact us."

"Well, maybe Keith will be out there and we can talk to him again," Ryan said.

"You haven't looked yet?" Hagan asked.

"I haven't been awake long," Ryan answered.

"You don't look like you are yet," Hagan said.

"It is taking me a while to get there," Ryan said.

"Anything preventing you from sleeping or causing you to wake up at times during the night?" Hagan asked.

"No," Ryan answered, "I had a couple drinks last night on my way home and I stayed out later than I probably should have, but I didn't want to come straight home with the man in the suit following me. Even if he already knows where I live."

"It is instinct," Hagan said, "Nothing strange when you arrived home?"

"I didn't find anything," Ryan answered, "But I also didn't stop at the grocery store because I stopped elsewhere. I left my window open instead."

"You are going to have to find some other time to go grocery shopping," Hagan said.

"Likely," Ryan said.

"I'll go see if Keith is outside," Hagan said as he got to his feet. Ryan sipped his coffee while he waited. Hagan came back a moment later.

"He isn't out there," Hagan said as he sat back down, "But neither is the man in the suit who was following you yesterday."

"Anyone suspicious?" Ryan asked.

"There were a few I wouldn't trust based on my observations, but not in the way you mean," Hagan answered.

"Good to know," Ryan said with a nod. He took another sip of coffee. Hagan took out his phone, he dialled the number from yesterday, and put the phone to his ear. After waiting for several minutes and not getting a response, Hagan hung up.

"So, now what?" Ryan asked.

"I'm working on that," Hagan answered, "I asked my guy if he could trace it or tell me anything about the other end. He couldn't find any information. If it didn't ring on the other end, he would have claimed it didn't connect to anything."

"It has to go somewhere," Ryan said, "He can't trace it to any locations?"

"He couldn't," Hagan answered, "But he was going to try something else to see if he could find a physical location. I will check with him this evening to see if he has found something useful."

Before Hagan could say anything more, there was a knock on the apartment door. Ryan got up and went to the door. He looked through the peephole and saw Keith. Ryan opened the door and let Keith inside. Then they went to the kitchen. Keith sat down.

"Coffee?" Ryan asked.

"No, thank you," Keith answered, "I already had a couple of cups today."

"Did you find anything for us?" Hagan asked.

"It is a military thing," Keith answered, "Unfortunately, my access to their systems are limited. The ethernet is really meant to keep people out and it also keeps us in."

"Well, thank you for trying," Ryan said.

"I'm not finished yet," Keith said, "I got caught trying to get into files that might have given me some information. I was surprised when they didn't fire me right there. Instead, I was given a meeting with a General Blakely, who wanted to know what I was doing and why. I explained that I was looking for information for you and that I had seen the agents."

"Somehow. I doubt this will end well," Hagan said, "Usually, once the confessions start, things go downhill."

"He offered you a meeting with the person in charge of that department," Keith said, "I said I would have to ask you."

"If we enter the meeting room, will we be able to leave?" Hagan asked.

"As far as I know," Keith answered, "But I am only a bystander and if I want to keep my job, I have to back off once I offer you this."

Ryan could see Hagan was mulling it over and very suspicious of it. It did not sound especially friendly or safe to agree to. Ryan was concerned about taking the offer himself. His brain was screaming at him to avoid what could only be a trap, but his heart spoke its small voice. It wanted to see Abigail again; to hold her in his arms and see her on the other side of the bed.

"We will go to the meeting," Ryan said. Hagan looked at him for a long moment. Ryan thought Hagan figured him to be still waking up, but then something changed in Hagan's eyes.

"Okay," Hagan said, "Yes, we will go to this meeting."

"I will let them know," Keith said as he took out his phone. He got up and left the kitchen before dialling the number.

"Are you sure?" Hagan asked.

"No," Ryan answered, "But if this gets me to Abby, I am willing to do it."

"That makes sense," Hagan said, "All of our other

leads have run out, so this might be our chance."

"Then I really hope this works out," Ryan said.

"I have people who will look for me if I disappear," Hagan said, "And I advertise that fact, so they will know that. I don't know about you."

"Tony knows about my mission and will start to ask questions," Ryan said, "Abby's best friend, Savanna, knows about it as well. I doubt she would do much to rock the boat though."

"Then it seems unlikely we will disappear without someone asking after us," Hagan said, "That is a good thing."

Ryan nodded. He was not entirely sure about this whole thing, but he was the one who was determined to find his girlfriend. Hagan was being paid for his role. Ryan wondered why Hagan had not asked to be paid the rest before the meeting; though that could still be coming. Keith came back into the kitchen and sat down.

"He seemed glad you accepted the meeting," Keith said, "The meeting is at the Terry Munchlier building at one-thirty this afternoon."

"Doesn't give us very long," Hagan said checking his watch.

"They wouldn't want to give us too much time," Ryan said.

"Then you will have to excuse me," Hagan said as he started to get up, "I have a couple things I need to do before the meeting. I will see you on the steps of the building twenty minutes before the meeting."

"See you then," Ryan said.

Hagan left the apartment without Ryan showing him out. Keith stayed seated.

"I am sorry I couldn't get you more without getting

in trouble," Keith said.

"It is okay," Ryan said, "This meeting is somewhat of what we wanted. Not quite the way we wanted, but close enough. I really hope you don't get into too much trouble for being caught looking for the information."

"I will have to behave for a while until they forget about it," Keith said, "If they were going to fire me, they would have already done it."

"Are there agents out front today?" Ryan asked.

"No," Keith answered, "Most likely, they were pulled from that duty when the meeting was set up. They would be back after you turned it down."

"Nice to know I don't have to worry about them today," Ryan said, "Yesterday was tiring with the agent following me."

"Well, I should get back," Keith said, "I really hope it all goes well for you."

"Thank you," Ryan said. They got up and went to the door. Keith left and Ryan locked the door behind him. Knowing time was limited, Ryan went back to the kitchen to have another cup of coffee and make himself some lunch.

The taxi was waiting on the curb when Ryan stepped out of his apartment and locked the door. He went down and got inside.

"Good afternoon, sir," the taxi driver from the night before said.

"Good afternoon," Ryan said, "Nice to see you again."

"Good to see you are well, sir," the taxi driver said, "Where to?"

"The Terry Munchlier building," Ryan answered.

"The government building?" the taxi driver asked, "Very well, sir." He pulled away from the curb and into traffic.

"Are you married?" Ryan asked.

"I am not, sir," the taxi driver answered, "But I am engaged."

"Would you do anything for her?" Ryan asked.

"I would, sir," the taxi driver answered.

"She may only be my girlfriend," Ryan said, "And I would too. That is what this is all about."

"Yes, sir," the driver said. There was some worry in his tone, but something about Ryan's voice seemed to keep him from asking further. Ryan fell into the quiet as he watched out the window. It was still the state-mate quiet in which they arrived at the building. The driver pulled to the curb. Ryan paid the fare.

"Good luck, sir," the driver said.

"Thank you," Ryan said, "Have a good day." He got out of the taxi and headed up the steps. Hagan was already waiting beside the door. They went inside together. There was a counter across the lobby preventing anyone from going farther into the building without them being allowed inside. Hagan led the way to the lady at the counter.

"Yes?" the woman asked.

"We have a meeting with General Blakely," Hagan said, "I'm Hagan and he is Ryan White."

"Just a moment," the woman said. She picked up the phone beside her and hit a couple numbers and waited. She told the person who picked up the other end who was waiting and why. Then she listened. When they were finished, she put the phone down and looked up at them.

"Someone will be down in a moment," she told them.

"Okay," Hagan said. He and Ryan stepped away from the counter and waited. They did not speak anything as neither had much to say. It was several minutes of waiting before someone came in sight. He was dressed in a military uniform. The rank visible is Warrant Officer. As he came closer the patch with his name read Mandel. He came over to them.

"Please follow me," Warrant Officer Mandel said.

"Lead on," Hagan said. Warrant Officer Mandel nodded and then turned on his heel. He went back the way he had come. Hagan and Ryan followed. They went passed the counter and into the other side of the building. There were two elevators on the wall but Warrant Officer Mandel did not stop. Instead, he went to a door marked stairs. Hagan and Ryan continued to follow him.

They went through the door. However, instead of heading up the stairs, Warrant Officer Mandel opened the door with the exit sign pointing to it and held it open. Outside in the alley was a black van with the back doors open. Hagan and Ryan did not even glance at each other before going through the door and climbing into the back of the van. There were two more men in uniform already inside, but with the only light coming in through the windshield it was impossible to see rank or names. Ryan and Hagan made themselves as comfortable as they could. Warrant Officer Mandel closed the doors from the outside.

The van started moving. Hagan kept an eye out from where they were going. Ryan did not bother. Neither man in uniform bothered to try and stop Hagan from looking out front. The van was driving like it was in the city with a slower speed and the stops and starts for traffic lights. There were a few turns. Even if Ryan had been trying to keep track of where they were, he would be confused now. Since he rarely went places by car and when he did he was not driving, Ryan really did not know the city well enough to know where they were or where they might be heading.

The van pulled into someplace dark that had some bumpy area before it smoothed out. It felt like an enclosed space and even in the van Ryan could feel the echo quality. Hagan gave no indication he had noticed any changes or seen any. However, Ryan could tell that he was still awake and watching. The van tipped forward as if going down a slope and it did not level out for several minutes. When it did, the van stopped briefly. Outside there was the sound of something heavy, like a rock, moving. Once the sound has stopped, the van moved forward again. It got darker inside the van.

Ryan could barely see Hagan and the uniformed man. He was not sure how the driver could see where to go. Hagan was still looking out the front window, Ryan was sure he had not seen Hagan move. The van was moving at a steady speed and on level terrain. The sound of the van echoed off close walls, but that was not the only thing Ryan could hear. Somewhere nearby, there was running water and he could hear it slightly over the sounds of the van. He half wanted to ask Hagan if he could hear it too, but with the two uniformed men in the van Ryan felt it better to not say anything.

Ryan did not want to give away anything he saw or

heard if it gave the men information about what Ryan knew. Maybe Hagan's paranoia was wearing off on Ryan, or maybe Ryan's natural paranoia was kicking up. Or it was sitting in a van with two military men going through a dark tunnel after being getting in by the back door of a government building. Not to mention everything that Hagan had dug up about Abigail's past and the men in suits following Ryan for the last while. The one thing keeping Ryan from panicking was the thought they had not tried to kill him yet. It was not a heartwarming thought, but it was enough to keep him calm.

On the other hand, Ryan might actually find Abigail. That had been the object of this quest. He would get to see her and maybe, hopefully, he would be able to hug her. He was not sure about getting her away from the government, but he would consider that when the time came to figure it out. Maybe he could just make a deal with them and they could let Abigail stay with him while she worked for them. He doubted it because otherwise, they would not have kidnapped her. But right now, Ryan felt an optimism about the whole situation and where it was headed.

Ryan was not sure how long they had been travelling, but the van was now slowing down. The van turned a corner but did not speed up again. Instead, it slowed down even further. It turned again and then stopped. The engine was turned off and the uniformed men shifted to get out of the van. Ryan and Hagan did the same. The back door was opened by a man dressed the same. It was light enough that Ryan could see the man was ranked a Warrant Officer and a name patch that read J. Golden.

"Follow me," Warrant Officer Golden said.

"Okay," Ryan said as he got out of the van. Hagan followed him out. Both of the uniformed men did the same. The van was parked in a lot with three other dark vans. The whole place was a concrete bunker with limited lighting. Warrant Officer Golden went passed all the vehicles to a metal door with an hand-pad beside it. Warrant Officer Golden put his hand on the pad and after a moment, there was a click and he pulled the door open. He went through first and the others followed. The last man closed the door.

Inside was more concrete with fluorescent lighting in a long row in the ceiling. It felt cold, impersonal, and secure. At the end of this hallway, it split into a t and Warrant Officer Golden took them to the left. This hallway had three doors off it; two in the middle and one at the very end. Warrant Officer Golden went to the right door and opened it. There was no security pad for this room. Ryan and Hagan followed Warrant Officer Golden into the room. The other two did not and the door was left to swing shut.

This room was a conference room with a table taking up most of it. There were office chairs set all around it. At one end was a screen mounted on a wall. The table at that end had a telephone on it as well as a keyboard and remote. Along the wall opposite the door was a large whiteboard.

"Have a seat," Warrant Officer Golden said.

Ryan and Hagan picked two chairs in the middle of the table on the same side as the door. They sat down. Warrant Officer Golden took up a post beside the door.

"Will it be a long wait?" Hagan asked.

"No, Mr. Hagan, it will not be," a man answered

from the doorway. Ryan and Hagan turned to look because they had not heard the door open. The man stepped inside and strode to the chair at the head of the table. He sat down and put his hands flat on the table in front of him. His eyes seemed to burn into both Ryan and Hagan as they stared back. This man was also in uniform but his rank was a colonel.

"I am Colonel Curtroth," the man said, "And I know exactly who you are."

"You run this place?" Hagan asked.

"I do," Colonel Curtroth said with a nod.

"We were told we were meeting a General Blakely," Hagan said.

"General Blakely is a false name used as a buffer between this place and the rest of the government," Colonel Curtroth said, "We used it on Mr. Benson to avoid him knowing too much as he seemed keen to avoid losing his job."

"So, what is this place?" Hagan asked.

"It was formerly called the Platt Truman Institution," Colonel Cutroth answered, "And that was long before the school aspect existed. I prefer not to give you the current name due to you becoming security risks."

"Then, you don't consider us ones now?" Hagan asked.

"Since you will never return here and you can't get back on your own, no," Colonel Cutroth answered, "All the information I will provide to you will also not cause you to be security risks."

"Let's hear this information," Hagan said, "Since I am assuming that you are not going to give us the full history of Platt Truman School for Exceptional Students and why you were abducting children to go there."

"It was a government program in response to similar programs of other countries," Colonel Cutroth said, "I was not in command at that time, however, most of the children brought to the institute were not abducted. They were here with the permission of their parents. When it came to children who were in foster care, money was exchanged in some cases."

"And parents were bumped off for easy access," Hagan said.

"No, parents were never killed," Colonel Cutroth said, "It was a coincidence if parents were killed. In the case of Selena Stafferson, which was the one you were looking into, the death of her parents had nothing to do with the institute. It was also long before she came to our attention."

"But she did have family," Ryan said.

"Based on the case notes, it was not known that she had a brother," Colonel Curtroth said, "It is only recently we learned of the matter. Had we known at the time, he would have been told what happened to her."

"She has been running from you for many years," Ryan said.

"Unfortunately, that is true," Colonel Cutroth said, "She was part of an important project, which is still going, and the information she has is highly classified. We were concerned about both matters. Our attempts to contact her were met with resistance, so the options were limited. However, she is once again a resident of the institute and will not be leaving until the project is finished."

"So, you kidnapped her and are keeping her against her will," Hagan said.

"She is not being kept against her will," Colonel Cutroth said, "If you ask her, she will tell you that she is happy here. Unfortunately, the men who brought her back in did not leave the important note the first time. So, we sent it out later in hopes it would help clear up the matter."

"It might if it even resembled something she would write," Ryan said, "But it didn't."

"Can we speak with to find out if she is happy?" Hagan asked.

"You cannot," Colonel Curtroth answered, "It would be a security issue."

"May I see her?" Ryan asked.

"I suppose that is possible," Colonel Curtroth answered, "But only you."

"Thank you," Ryan said. Hagan nodded his acceptance.

"Follow me," Colonel Curtroth said as he stood up. Ryan got up and hurried to follow Colonel Curtroth, who was already at the door. Warrant Officer Golden did not move from his position, not even to open the door. Colonel Curtroth exited the room and went to the left. Ryan followed him back down the hallway and back to the t intersection. But they went straight this time. It was fairly short before turning to the left. This was a much longer hallway. At the end were two doors. One was at the end and the other was slightly down on the right. Both had hand-pads next to them.

Colonel Curtroth put his hand to the door on the right. The lock clicked and he opened the door. Ryan followed him through. Colonel Curtroth closed the door and only then did the lights come on. This space was also concrete. It was a small space with a metal staircase heading up into a doorway. It was almost like the doorways were built and then someone realized there was no way to access one from the other, so they put the staircase in.

Ryan followed Colonel Curtroth up the stairs and into the next room. It was an observation room. It was long with a counter on one side, a couple chairs, and a window on that side of the room. The window was tinted so whoever was inside could not see who was watching them. Colonel Curtroth went to stand where the room below was visible. Ryan stopped beside him and looked down.

It was another concrete room. This one was large and almost looked like barracks. There were two rows of beds on each side. Each bed had a locker at the end of it. The beds were the most basic model and the blankets were the thin type popular in institutions because they were cheap. The door had another hand-pad on the inside to prevent people from being able to get out. There were no personal items visible anywhere and nothing up on the walls. It was not home to anyone. Most of the beds were made as if their occupants were missing.

Ryan's eyes were drawn to the only person in the room. It was Abigail. She was sitting on a bed reading a book. Her hair was pulled back in a ponytail. The ends were still blonde. She was wearing a black t-shirt, military pants, and black socks. There was a pair of boots beside the bed. Ryan could not see the title of the book she was reading, but it had the appearance of a text.

Seeing her filled Ryan was the love he felt for her and the pain in his chest of missing her was there. It was like he was filled and empty all at once. He craved wrapping her in his arms and keeping her there for the rest of his life. There were a couple problems with that. One was standing next to him and another was a couple doors with hand-pads. Ryan knew he was not powerful enough to take on the man standing next to him.

Abigail seemed to know she was being watched as she shifted slightly. She did not look up from her book, but her eyes did stop briefly. Ryan could feel the urge to call out her. He squished it as it would not do either of them any good. The observation room was likely soundproof and Colonel Curtroth would likely prevent Ryan from doing anything. Ryan figured that Colonel Curtroth was giving him this look at Abigail hoping that Ryan would give up the search because this was the show that Abigail was in good health.

"As you can see, Selena is fine," Colonel Curtroth said.

"I can see that," Ryan said. He had tried to keep emotion from his voice but he was not as successful as he hoped.

"I suppose there are a few things I should mention about the program," Colonel Curtroth said, "One is that she is necessary for the project and there is no way to so-call rescue her."

"And what else?" Ryan asked without looking at Colonel Curtroth because that would mean taking his eyes off Abigail.

"If you tried to take her away, she wouldn't leave with you," Colonel Curtroth said.

"And why would that be?" Ryan asked.

"Because she doesn't remember you," Colonel Curtroth answered, "When she arrived here, she made it clear to everyone that for this project to be finished she would need to have the last several years wiped. That is what we did. Now she has no memory of you. If you met her on the street, she would see you as a stranger. The best thing you can do for you, for her, and for Mr. Hagan is to leave Selena here and move on with your life."

Ryan stared down at Abigail. She was back to reading as if she was not worried about anyone who might be watching her. Ryan had come all this way to find her and here she was. Colonel Curtroth had admitted that she had not left him of her own free will without even a note of explanation. No, she has been kidnapped and her memory erased. Ryan had found his perfect ten.

To be Continued.......

ABOUT THE AUTHOR

Heather Mantler is a lover of fairy tales and fables. Her home town is Prince George, British Columbia. Heather is always working on another story as she hopes to finish every story idea that she has ever written down. She was a nominee for the fiction category of the 2012 Prince George Regional Arts and Cultural Awards and short listed for the 2013 John Harris Fiction Awards. Her blog is heathersdomain.wordpress.com. Heather encourages her readers to post reviews on Good Reads and Amazon.

www.ingramcontent.com/pod-product-compliance
Lightning Source LLC
Chambersburg PA
CBHW022119170626
46808CB00002B/771